I0788228

For Cale

Always

LEGENDS

~~BYRON BRONZEBOW~~ DEAD

A good-looking hero who carries a bronze bow. Known in history for his care for the poor and needy.

DEATHLESS PIRATE

Known for his love of treasure and invulnerability and recognized by his hook for a hand and belt of human skulls.

GRANDFATHER TIMELESS

Based in the Timekeepers religion he is known for his high hat, long black coat and golden waistcoat. He is Time in human form subjecting all to his will.

~~King Abelmeyer the One-Eyed~~ DEAD

Known for his single eye and broken crown, King Abelmeyer united the five cities of the Dragonblood Plains in the alliance that lasts today.

~~LADY SACRIFICE~~ DEAD

Known for her loveliness, innocence and sacrifice for the people, she is usually clad in a white dress.

LILA CHERRYLOCKS

A master thief and trickster. Known for her long cherry-red locks, deft skills, and adventurous spirit.

MAID CHAOS (REBORN)

The right hand of Death. Known for destruction, death and the golden breastplate she wears.

~~QUEEN MER~~ DEAD

Queen of the Sea and mother to the Waverunners. Queen Mer is known for her revenge upon man in the form of hurricanes and typhoons and for the shells, scales, and seaweed that she wears.

RAM THE HUNTER

The unspoken Legend. Not mentioned in the Dragonblood Plains except in whispers, he is known for slaying dragons and going insane in the aftermath.

THE ADMIRAL

New Legend added by the Retribution in Choan.

BRIDGE of LEGENDS
HEI
HAI
YAN
XIN
JING
JINGEN
Districts
Alchemist
Governement
Temple
University
Spice
Artificer
Trade

Prologue

"Death, the great equalizer of men, stalks our steps, shadows our thoughts, and mimics our hopes. So that in the end, only by embracing its cold touch may we ever be free of its tyranny."

- Tales of the Dragonblooded

SPRINGHATCH

A SEASON OF CELEBRATION

1: Running Water

MARIELLE

Marielle gripped the sides of the boat as Jhinn called commands from the rear.

"Hold on to something!" he called.

The water had changed directions as soon as they outdistanced the pull of the portal, and with the removal of half the mountain range – since those mountains had been trapped dragons, which were now free – the water all flowed downhill and very quickly.

Tamerlan held an oar and stood in the front of the gondola, using an oar to shove them away from any large rock or piece of debris as they rushed down the angry river.

Etienne looked equally tense as he held the other oar and used it to steer as Jhinn commanded. Jhinn was manning the pedal assembly, refusing to let anyone else take a turn at the pedals, and angrily ordering Tamerlan and Etienne as they worked. He hadn't let up since the moment they turned their backs on the portal and Marielle could almost see the strain of it in his face – as if the portal was calling him back even as he fled in the other direction.

His scent was a tangled mess of hope and anxiety – smoked paprika and morning dew fighting for dominance.

She understood why. There was nothing he wanted more than the culmination of his life coming true in the waters of the worlds between worlds. And yet, he couldn't leave his people ignorant of the fact that what they'd hoped for all their lives was finally becoming real.

If only Marielle's news was so sweet and hopeful. When she reached the plains, she would have her own message to deliver, but it was hardly the good news of a great hope. It was the grim warning to flee every city before she made them each uninhabitable. If the people there knew what she was going to do – if Etienne or Tamerlan knew – then they'd try to stop her with everything they had. It had to remain a secret until the right time. Until then, she could only trust Jhinn.

Which was the first of her problems. She needed to get to the back of the dragon H'yi – the very dragon they'd fled just days ago – and smash Grandfather Timeless' clock before that dragon flew again. It was the only way to free her next potential ally. Until then, she couldn't trust Etienne. Even now, she could see the gleam in his eyes as he watched her. Was that him or the Legend inside him looking at her that way?

If only there was a sure way to get a dragon to sit still. She frowned thinking about it. Had she seen that happen before?

Yes, she realized, blanching at the thought. Tamerlan had used Abelmeyer's Eye to bring a dragon down. It had only held him a few months, but he'd done it. But to use it, he'd given up use of one eye. And she still wasn't even sure how he'd made the exchange.

She swallowed roughly and edged toward the front of the gondola. Tamerlan leaned forward, shoving the nose of the gondola away from a sharp black rock. They heaved away from it, foam and spray spilling over the sides of the boat.

Marielle laid a hand on Tamerlan's arm and he flinched and then immediately moved the oar as if to distract from his movements. It was hard not to let his reaction gut her – even knowing it was the Legends and not Tamerlan. His golden scent washed over her, laced with cranberry guilt.

"Marielle," he said gently, offering her a small smile. He was still himself sometimes. But who would listen to her plea? Him or Ram the Hunter? Or another Legend?

She would have to be careful how she worded it. She didn't want to deceive him. Not until she had to.

"Tamerlan, do you still have Abelmeyer's Eye?"

He flinched again, this time his hand moving to his chest. Did he have it under his shirt? Somehow that sounded like him – to run around the countryside with a priceless gem under his shirt. His expression hardened.

"Did you use it before to bring down the dragon Jingen?" she asked, but she didn't have to ask. His one eye – the one that turned a little more opaque every day – was all the evidence she needed that he had given an eye to do that. Besides, he'd screamed that at her only hours ago.

"Yes," he rasped and this time the suspicious slit-eyed look on his face was certainly not his own. Neither was that Elderflower scent of insanity. One of the Legends had his ear right now. His hands around the oar were white-knuckled, as if he was fighting an internal battle.

"If I needed to bring down another dragon and hold him in place, do you think it would work again?" she asked.

This time there was no mistaking how his hand clutched at his chest. "You just set a hundred dragons free, and now you're talking about trapping one." His words were light, but she heard the warning behind them. "Even if you did want to trap one, I told you before that I am fighting to keep you out of this battle. Why should you lose an eye, also?"

His voice throbbed with pain at the end of his statement and she felt a stab of fear. He was going through so much! But if she didn't end this somehow – and quickly – the Legends within him would destroy him from the inside out.

"And you promised to trust me," she reminded him.

He turned a look on her that broke her heart. A look half of desperation and half of hope. There was no residue of a Legend in it at all. The colors of that scent tangled around him – orange and bronze.

"Of course," he said, shaking his head as if he couldn't believe he'd ever resisted her.

He reached in his collar and pulled out the amulet with the single ruby at the center – Abelmeyer's Eye. "Please, take it."

That earnestness – those deep blue eyes and trembling lips – she just wanted to save him from this. She wanted to tuck him away somewhere safe and wake him when it was over. But it didn't work like that. Couldn't work like that. She had an entire world to save – and she doubted anyone in it was going to make this easy for her. Even her own allies were as likely to turn on her as strangers if she didn't play this just right. But the eye was the first step. After all, the Legends wouldn't suspect a thing if she seemed to be on their side, would they?

She smelled a sudden puff of suspicion and spun to see Etienne glaring at her, suspicion leaving a trail behind him that stained the river stone grey. Of course. Ram the Hunter might be fine with her having the eye – especially if that meant lulling a dragon to sleep – but what would Grandfather Timeless think of it? Could he possibly suspect what she hoped to do to one of the only two dragons roaming free? Or why she might need to do it before he ever suspected?

She held the amulet, staring at the ruby in the center. How did you even use something like this?

YOU PLAN TO BETRAY US?

She jumped at the voice of the dragons in her head, echoing as if from far away.

No! She wasn't trying to betray them. But she had to make H'yi sit still long enough to do something about the Grandfather on his back. As long as the Legends lived, the dragons were tied to them. Which meant that every single Legend had to be destroyed to free the dragons. Or was she wrong about that?

YOU ARE NOT WRONG.

That meant she needed H'yi to sit still for long enough to get in the city and to the clock.

YOU COULD JUST ASK.

Ask the dragon? Yes, that would work out. He'd been so accommodating the last time they'd tried to hold him down.

WE WILL ASK.

The water around them was flowing more quickly and Marielle wiped spray from her eyes. They'd been in this narrow rock channel for a while now. Tt flowed between two mountains, never branching. But they were still at a high elevation. How long could this channel keep going?

She looked back at Jhinn. His face was white and worried as he looked ahead.

"I think we need to stop and one of you needs to scout ahead," he said. "The water is speeding up and I have a bad feeling about this."

"The river is the fastest way to the lowlands," Etienne replied. he had to raise his voice. The sound of the water was growing stronger. "Walking out would take months and we have no supplies."

Which would be deadly considering it was winter in the mountains. Here in the river, the water was running and it hadn't frozen over, though the edges of the river had a foot of ice stretching out toward the center. Bright blue ice that looked like it could cut you, the edge was so sharp. Etienne was right that this was the only way out.

WE HAVE FOUND THE DRAGON H'YI. HE WILL ALLOW YOU TO ACCESS HIS BACK. BUT YOU WILL NEED TO WORK QUICKLY. HE IS ANGRY AND IN GREAT PAIN. HE MAY ACT UNPREDICTABLY.

Great. An unpredictable dragon. Just what she'd always wanted.

"It's not a matter of how to reach the lowlands," Jhinn said. Was he shouting now? "I'm more worried about the waterfall."

"Waterfall?" Fear filled Etienne's eyes, puffing up in lightning-blue clouds and then he was looking at the steep cliff faces on either side - the cliff faces that had gotten steeper as they spoke - so steep and slick that there was no way you could climb them - especially as they were coated with a shining skim of ice.

"Why do you think I've been warning you that we need to stop?" Jhinn yelled.

Etienne cursed, by Marielle was shaking her head. There was no way to stop. There was nowhere to grab a hold of. No options except to keep going.

H'YI IS CLOSE. HE WILL MEET YOU. WE TRACK YOUR MIND.

Well, that might be hard to arrange since she was about to go over a waterfall. Her gaze met Tamerlan's and they shared a look of understanding, of pain, of bitter hope. Marielle took a step forward and took his hand, thrilling for a moment at the way his face relaxed when she held it. They had that much at least – a bond of trust that ran deep through their shared pains and guilt. He drew his oar into the boat.

"Oars in. Motor up. Get low!" Jhinn commanded from the back, working to strap his motor into the boat. "Tie in!"

Tamerlan drew Marielle down and together they tied the rope at the front of the boat around their waists. They were certainly going to die. The moments seemed to drag out as if Marielle's brain was trying to live every one of them as quickly as possible. She gripped Tamerlan's hand, trying to keep her expression calm and reassuring instead of panicked, but her thoughts were a maddening swirl of fear.

On a whim, she pulled her head up and leaned against the ferro so she could see. The gondola turned a corner and ahead of her the river just stopped and there was only sky and clouds beyond that point and a fine mist of water in the air that made particles dance in a rainbow just above the surface of the water. They were going to die in style.

"I'm glad I knew you, Tamerlan," Marielle said. "I want you to know," she hesitated a moment, but there was no time to second-guess. "I love you."

And he leaned in, pressing a cheek to hers and then kissed her forehead like a man drinking water for the last time. It was a goodbye like the goodbye of the sun before it was eclipsed by the stormclouds.

The gondola seemed to tip for a moment and then they were falling through the frosty air. Marielle thought she might be screaming. The water plunged below them through a drop higher than she could have imagined - even having flown on the back of a dragon. It went on and on and on, the trees on the banks below looking like tiny miniatures.

And then suddenly, eclipsing the sight, the blackened and burned body of a dragon suddenly burst under the fall of water, the water pouring over its back, spreading out across the ruined city streets and buildings there. Behind her, Etienne was screaming something. She didn't know what. And then the buildings were right there. They were going to hit one - or failing that, hit the street under the water.

And then the gondola plunged beneath the waves and the ferro she was holding was gone, the breath *whooshing* out of her lungs. Coldness shattered her thoughts and water swirled all around her in clouds of bubbles so erratic that they blurred her vision. She tried to hold her breath but there was nothing to hold and she sucked in water that burned, burned, burned. Something pulled her. Air hit her face like a blow. She coughed, expelling water everywhere, her lungs screaming, her eyes blinded by streams of water.

Her hands clawed out and met fabric and she clutched it, coughing and heaving, curled over herself like a mollusk as she tried to squeeze every drop of burning water from her lungs. Someone was murmuring to her.

"That's right. Get it all up. There you go. Just breathe, sweet Marielle, just breathe." Hands gently drew her dripping hair back from her face and then gathered her shivering body in, in, in.

She blinked and looked up into ice blue eyes and blue lips. Tamerlan was shaking in the cold just like she was. She looked around. They were on the hull of the gondola. It was upside down and Jhinn was in the water, holding the gondola with one hand and the edge of a bridge with the other.

He coughed in the water, his movements slowed by the cold.

"We need to flip it over and assess the damage," he said through thick lips. "Can you stand on the bridge, Marielle?"

She scrambled across the hull, her wet clothing hindering her movements, grabbed the railing and pulled herself up. It was a sturdy bridge made of rock and stonework and she could see how it lasted when so much else didn't, but the strength was leeching out of her in the cold and she was struggling to think coherent thoughts.

THE DRAGON H'YI HAS AGREED TO GIVE YOU FOUR HOURS TO FIND YOUR CLOCK AND DO WHAT YOU MUST.

She froze, her hands and feet trembling, panic surging through her. Four hours? That was all? She spun in place, looking at the unfamiliar city. Nothing looked the same half-submerged under flowing water. She wouldn't even know how to get to the clock, never mind what to do once she was there.

She didn't even know how they'd survived the drop.

WE ASKED H'YI TO SEND OUT HIS STRENGTH TO SHELTER YOU.

Magic? She felt like laughing. He'd saved them with magic? That seemed a little too convenient.

SHOULD WE ASK HIM NOT TO SPARE YOU NEXT TIME?

Steps pounded down the bridge and Etienne arrived beside her, soaking wet and gasping.

"Magic," he said, and he stank of it – the heady, vanilla and lilac scent of it swirling around her like warmth would if only she had any to find. "It was magic that kept us alive – but whose or how – I don't know."

In the water below, Tamerlan and Jhinn heaved and the gondola flipped over. The ferro and lantern from the front of the boat had snapped off and the oars were gone, but the motor Jhinn had made was still there, strapped in place.

Jhinn started bailing immediately. There was still eight inches of water inside the gondola.

Tamerlan pulled himself up onto the bridge, water flowing from his heavy clothing.

"We need to get warm somehow before we freeze to death," he said.

"I don't have time for that," Marielle said. "We have four hours before the dragon moves. Four hours to do what we need to do and leave."

"Leave?" Tamerlan seemed shocked.

Etienne raised a single eyebrow. "The drop from the dragon's back to the ground is just as far as it was from the top of the water to his back. We might not survive that drop."

"Perhaps he will set us down on the ground," Marielle said.

Etienne's eyes narrowed. "Why is he clinging to the cliffside, Marielle? Why did he catch us at all?"

She swallowed. His fists were clenched. If the Grandfather suspected … even for a moment …

She shook her head to clear the thought. Even thinking it might be too much.

"Listen, there's something I need to do," she said through chattering teeth. "I just need a bit of time to do it. You men stay here and I'll be back in a few hours."

"Absolutely not," Tamerlan said, his eyes on her chest. She started to blush until she realized he was looking at the lump under her shirt where the amulet was. She hadn't needed it to still the dragon. But he must still suspect what she might do with a thing like that. Maybe it had enough power to destroy the clock.

"We will go with you. Jhinn will take care of the boat." Etienne turned to Jhinn. "You'll survive until then?"

Jhinn nodded stiffly. His attention was on clearing the boat of water, but his eyes kept drifting to his motor. Was he worried that it hadn't survived the fall? His anxious scent could mean anything. They all smelled heavily of that smoked paprika, ochre trails swirling around them.

"It would be best if you stayed here," Marielle said to Etienne. She needed some reason for him to stay. Some reason to keep the Grandfather as far away as possible. She bit the inside of her lip, thinking. "You should gather wood and find a brazier. We'll need a fire, so we don't freeze to death."

"If this dragon moves or if we try to go over the falls to the river below, we'll die faster than hypothermia can kill us," Etienne objected, his eyes glittering dangerously. He suspected. She was sure of it.

"It's best that we spilt up," she said.

"Fine." He seemed torn, his face clouding like he was trying to work out a problem in his head.

"Come on, Tamerlan," Marielle said, grabbing his sleeve and pulling before anyone could reconsider. If she didn't get moving now, then she'd lose her chance. And perhaps Tamerlan could help. He'd used the Eye once. Maybe he could coach her to use it again if that was the only way to bring down the tower.

2: ICE AND WATER

Tamerlan followed Marielle with an icy hand gripping his heart.

Now, Ram said in his mind. *You're alone now. Grab her and drag her into one of these buildings and I will show you how to form her into the perfect avatar to bind this dragon!*

His hand was twitching to obey. He swallowed down bile at the feeling. He was shaking already, not from the cold, but from fear. If his self-control failed for even a moment, he might find his own hands destroying the woman he loved.

Anything to stop the dragons. I will sacrifice my own soul. My loved ones. My life.

That was Ram. Ram! Not him.

He had to keep reminding himself of that. He had to hold on to the little scraps that were left of his mind as the Legend ravaged them and made them dance to his twisted tune.

"Where are we going?" he asked Marielle mildly. He needed something to hold on to. Something to think about other than what Ram was shouting.

"I can't tell you that," Marielle said, though she seemed very certain of her path, occasionally sniffing the air like she was scenting something. So much of the city was submerged by water that only the Temple, Government, and University districts seemed to have any dry land at all and even those streets were flooded in places, their canals choked to overflowing. Ahead of them, water washed across the street, waist-high in places.

"I will help you if I can," he said, but he tasted the lie in his words. He would help. But Ram would not. And he didn't dare smoke – not even for a moment. Ram would be sure to take hold of him if he did. And then all would be lost.

Ram is not the only Legend left. There had been a time when Lila's was the clearest voice he heard. Now, she was so faint he could barely pick out her voice. It wouldn't be her barreling over the Bridge if he opened it. It would be Ram. And Ram would sacrifice Marielle in a heartbeat.

She brought it on herself. Freeing dragons. Sacrificing humans. She is a witch and a traitor and you will be serving all mankind when you spread her out and make her body immortal and her soul bound to the Bridge and the Dragon.

He shivered. This was almost worse than when the Legends took his body. Now, they had taken his mind. He wasn't himself.

He might never be himself again.

Marielle stopped and put a hand on his arm. His heart broke at the kind look in her eyes. Broke because he knew he would fail her, even as it swelled with joy at her touch. He could hear the venom and death raging in his mind at the sight of her. He could feel his muscles tensing, ready to break her fragile body and wreck that beautiful golden trust she was offering him.

"Trust me, Tamerlan. I have a plan," she said simply. "But I can't tell it to you. Not now, and not even after this part is complete. Do you understand?"

He nodded. His tongue cleaving to the roof of his mouth and refusing to speak.

Don't agree with her! Her plans are nothing. It is our plans that matter.

Not theirs. Just Ram's. He refused to agree to the idea that they were a team. He'd do anything to protect Marielle.

Her life for thousands. A small price. A small choice. Only a villain would choose otherwise.

Then he was a villain. And he didn't care. He was already damned for the choices he'd made. Why not one more?

They were moving again, wading through waist-high water and then climbing upward again on the other side. Marielle was angling toward the Temple District. He shivered at the thought of that place. The place where he'd lost her to Grandfather Timeless, lost his eye, and then the place where he'd won her back and lost Liandari and Anglarok. She wasn't going back there again, was she?

If she tries to set him free, you will have to kill her at once. We don't dare let any Legend go free now. They must remain and do their duties! And we will make more. We will need many, many more …

No wonder they called him the Nameless Legend. No wonder he was shunned. He was a horror. Maid Chaos might revel in the death of innocents, but at least she had been mad. Ram the Hunter was sane as anyone and these choices of his were made of logic and duty – and yet they were more horrible than the madness of the Maid.

Don't speak to me of horrors. Do you know what will happen if you set them free?

They went through the portal. They were gone.

The laughter in his head – bitter and pained – hurt.

Gone for now. But the portal is open. They will be back, and they will slaughter innocents in your name. Do you want to watch children torn apart before their parents? Do you want to watch a man helpless as a dragon incinerates his wife and family? Do you want to hear a mother crying in the streets, her arms empty? Her children dead in a ruined building thanks to your dragon friends? Go ahead. Live that life. Live that agony. All because you were too weak to stop her. Too weak to make a single sacrifice.

He wanted to cry at the images that filled his mind. His chin trembled as he choked back tears. He hadn't realized that Ram could manufacture memories in his mind. That he could make Tamerlan see horrors that would not leave. He wanted to curl into a ball and sob until there was no more Tamerlan left, but the images didn't stop, didn't relent. His feet followed Marielle but his mind was tortured by Ram as the Legend whispered to him, *your fault, your fault, your fault.*

"Tamerlan?" Marielle's voice shocked him out of the memories, and he met her gaze with gratitude. Real. She was real. He stared at her like she could anchor him. She cleared her throat. "I need you to tell me how to use the Eye."

"Why?" he gasped. Was she going to trap the dragon like Ram wanted?

And then we bind her to it forever.

She was calm and certain as she spoke. "Tamerlan I need to destroy the cl – "

Her words cut off as Etienne leapt from the shadows and knocked her to the ground. The sound of bone hitting cobblestones jarred him.

He yelled through his teeth – a wordless roar – and charged.

Etienne!

He should have known there was something wrong with the man. He thought he could see the Grandfather – or his ghost – both inside and not inside Etienne, moving with him and through him. He grabbed the other man by the coat and lifted him off Marielle's prone body, throwing him through the air.

He blinked. Had he just done that? On his own? Without a Legend to help? He swallowed as Etienne hit the crystal casing of the clock and slid down the door of it to the ground.

Wait.

Tamerlan looked up. They were at the clock in H'yi where Marielle had been imprisoned. He blinked again. The sky was darkening. How many hours had they trudged through the cold and wet to get here? He looked around him, stunned, worried. He'd lost track of time. He had been lost in his own horrors. He felt like he was missing chunks of time completely. He blinked, stupefied, and looked at his hands. Had he been about to do something with them?

A body flew out of nowhere and knocked him off his feet. He landed in a puddle with a splash and the feeling of cold water seeped through his cloak and clothing.

He felt dazed but he clawed his way up in time to snatch his sword out of his scabbard just before a blade snaked toward him. The clash of his own sword against the other sword almost made him jump. What was happening to him?

Kill him! Kill the Grandfather!

He didn't bother ignoring that order. It sounded like good advice. He plunged forward, sword streaking out like a bolt of lightning toward his target. Etienne turned the blade cleverly, but the expression on his face – the deadly wickedness mixed with ancient malice – was not Etienne at all. The Grandfather had him.

Kill! Kill!

Tamerlan lunged again. Faster. Harder.

Again, his blade was turned. He spun into a defense and strangely, his body seemed to know what to do. It twirled to the side, his blade arm sweeping out and his wrist flicking so that Etienne's sword was turned away and jerked from his hand. It fell to the cobbles and rolled.

He almost smiled until Etienne scooped up a loose cobblestone from the street and flung it at him. There was barely time to dodge. He leapt to the side, nearly falling as his cloak tangled around his legs. He could hear the wind as the brick sped by. So close!

The other man was a wraith, moving rapidly so that Ram could hardly counter him. *Tamerlan* could hardly counter him.

Wait. Who was he?

Steel bit into flesh as his momentary lapse distracted him. He hissed, throwing his blade up just in time to deflect a follow-up strike. His left arm screamed in pain. Something there wasn't right.

He hadn't checked on Marielle before he'd begun to fight but he heard her moaning now and spared a glance in her direction. She held her head with one hand, stumbling to her feet.

Legends send she was okay! Legends send she hadn't hurt her brain it that fall!

We need her alive for the procedure. Funny that you still pray to us when you know what we are – and can unleash us at any moment.

He choked on the words but at that moment, Marielle jammed her hand against the clock and both Tamerlan and Etienne froze.

"Yes," Etienne gasped.

Ram flooded Tamerlan with pain, making his head spin. He turned to the side and vomited, wiping his mouth with the back of his hand.

He was losing his grip – on himself, on his thoughts, on everything.

But Marielle wasn't opening the clock. She pulled the amulet out of her shirt, grabbing it with the hand covered in blood from her fall.

Oh no. He couldn't remember how King Abelmeyer had used the Eye before – but he knew these things liked to activate with blood. And Marielle's blood was all over Abelmeyer's Eye now.

"No," he gasped. "Please don't!"

He'd done all this to save her from his fate. Why was she so intent on sacrificing herself? She was like a living Lady Sacrifice, constantly throwing herself at the flame. He bit the inside of his cheek, stumbling forward.

"No!" Etienne echoed him, but the panic in his voice was even stronger. He jumped toward her but mid-leap the world flashed white and disappeared.

Tamerlan tasted blood, blinking as his vision began to clear. Purple after-images danced across his vision. He didn't know how long he stood there blinking, but by the time he could see again, his body was numb from the cold, his feet heavy as bricks. He stumbled forward to where Marielle had collapsed on the ground, the clock behind her was melting toward her body. What kind of heat would melt a clock?

He sheathed his sword and lifted her in his numb hands, seconds before the molten glass and metal touched her body. She was soaking wet and cold to the touch. Was she … did she …

He was too scared to finish the sentence. He settled for clutching her to his chest, letting un-shed tears shake through him as he carefully backed away from what had once been a clock. He almost tripped over Etienne.

"Gone," the other man said. He was kneeling, his eyes fixed on the molten clock, the look of relief on his face so stark that Tamerlan could barely hold back the bitter jealousy raging through him. He knew immediately what the Lord Mythos meant by the word, "gone." He was free. The Legend that had held him was gone forever.

Tamerlan coughed, tasting blood through his lungs, his own heart ripping apart with more fury and jealousy than he realized he had. He didn't know how much of that was the red hot rage of Ram the Hunter inside him and how much was his own last desperate twitches as he tried to deny what he knew in his bones – that he was a dead man walking. That he would never walk free like Etienne. That his mind and body would be the price he paid for the freedom of everyone else – and the price he paid for the crime he committed when all of this started, and he called up Lila Cherrylocks in the smoke.

Absolution wasn't free.

Atonement had a price.

He was paying it in tears and blood and pain, and the full price wouldn't be paid until his life had been forfeited.

How had he ever thought otherwise? How had he ever dared to hope?

He stumbled through the ruined streets of H'yi, numb, the most precious person in the world in his arms. When he found Jhinn again, he was going to make him swear to bring her to safety. And he was going to make Etienne swear to keep her safe. But he couldn't stay near her. Not now that he knew the truth.

3: What Lies Beneath

Marielle woke to confusion. One of her eyes wasn't working. She rubbed it, blinking.

"Shh. It's going to be okay, Marielle," Tamerlan said. "You'll get used to it. It just feels strange at first."

With Tamerlan's words, her memories returned. She'd used the amulet. She'd destroyed the clock. Oh, sweet Legends, she'd given her eye for it! She gasped.

"Shh. It will be okay. It will," he said, comfortingly, rocking her as she hadn't been rocked since she was a tiny girl. But she could smell his anxiety mixing with the insanity of the Legends that was swirling around him thicker and thicker every moment. She clung to his golden scent of honey and lavender instead.

"How long," she said thickly. Swallowing and trying again. "How long have I been out?"

"An hour," Etienne said from nearby. She blinked her good eye – it was closest to Tamerlan's chest. Why wasn't it seeing correctly, either?

Oh. It was dark. A splashing sound met her ears. That explained the rocking. Tamerlan was carrying her. And Etienne was walking beside them.

"You should let me take a turn carrying her," Etienne said. "She's too heavy for you alone."

It sounded like an old argument. Like he didn't expect Tamerlan to listen.

"No," Tamerlan's words were firm. "I have her."

He stumbled slightly.

"I can walk," Marielle said, her voice fainter than she would have liked.

"You don't have to, Marielle." He said her name like he enjoyed it on his tongue and his head dipped for a moment and she felt the brush of his lips on the shell of her ear as his whisper tickled her ear. "I have you. I have you safe."

His golden scent was melting over her like hot honey running over her tongue. She would have liked to stay like that, to listen to his whispers and smell his tender scent.

There wasn't time for that.

"We only had four hours," she said, her voice still raspy. "Four hours until the dragon leaves and takes us with him. How many have already passed?"

The meaningful silence between Tamerlan and Etienne was worrying.

"How did you know there were only four hours?" Tamerlan asked in a choked voice. His grip around her felt tighter. Etienne was right in front of him before Marielle could blink, putting a hand on his shoulder.

"Easy Tamerlan. Easy. Maybe some things are better to keep from the Legends in your head, hmmm?"

She could feel Tamerlan tense at his words, but for once there was no edge to them. Did that mean that Etienne was free of the Grandfather as she'd hoped he would be? If he was, she would be able to trust him again. And she needed to be able to trust him. Her plan was too big for just her and Tamerlan. She needed someone else working to help her.

"I see Jhinn up ahead," Tamerlan said, breaking into their thoughts.

Ahead of them, something was glowing and as they strode toward the little boat Marielle saw a fire lit in a small brazier.

"You actually got him wood first?" Tamerlan asked Etienne. "I thought it was just a ruse so you could stalk us and attack us.

Etienne sounded superior as he replied. "I was able to do both."

The glow was tiny and far away, but Marielle could already feel the warmth of the fire on her skin as she drew in a long breath. Everything was going to be fine.

Her belly dropped and for a moment she thought Tamerlan had dropped her. She bit back a scream, but she could still feel his arms around her, tense and hard, could hear his quiet grunt and Etienne's bitter curse. The whole city was falling.

"Run," Tamerlan yelled to Etienne.

"Let me down!" Marielle demanded.

"Never." He was already running on soft, wobbling legs as they fell through the air with the whole city. The water surged across the streets and Tamerlan slipped, falling to the ground and grunting again.

Marielle scrambled out of his grip but took his hand. If he wasn't touching her at all he might panic – and besides, the world was spinning. She was having a hard time running with just one eye. She wasn't used to this at all.

"Hurry," Etienne choked out as they hit the freezing water, splashing and churning through it as it became waist-deep. "The lower the dragon gets, the more powerful the current!"

He was right. Marielle could barely keep her feet under her at all as it pushed against them. Tamerlan found a railing – the type that edged the canal – and grabbed it with his free hand, holding her in place as the current tried to pull her away. The water was rising. It was almost neck deep.

Etienne kicked through the current to grab the railing beside Tamerlan.

"I've lost sight of the glow," he gasped.

Marielle followed his gaze, her heart sinking when she saw he was right. What had happened to Jhinn and the gondola? Without him, they'd never get off H'yi's back before he rose into the air again and took them with him to the portal back up in the mountains.

She tried to scent for him, but all she could smell were their own panicked emotions swirling above the turgid waters.

Her heart was in her throat.

GO. NOW. OR LOSE YOUR CHANCE.

They were out of time.

A surge in the current tugged her so hard that she was ripped away from Tamerlan, pulled through the current and down the street more swiftly than they'd been running only moments before. She began to scream, but she only sucked in water. Tamerlan, Etienne and Jhinn were lost to her. She grabbed a signpost as she was swept by and held on for dear life. But why was she fighting the current at all? Why not just let it take her? She had already lost her companions and leaving this place now was her only hope left.

She was about to let go when out of nowhere the gondola appeared.

"Marielle!" Tamerlan called from the bow. He was soaking wet, Etienne beside him. Marielle couldn't make out Jhinn in the dark at all. Their scents were masked by the flowing water, misting and blanketing everything in the scent of living water.

"Here!" she called. "I'm here!"

Her grip slipped and she was whirled away again in the current, battered against stone buildings and swirled under the current and around again until she didn't know up from down.

She was going to die down here.

How long had she been under?

Her head broke the surface for a moment, and she took a breath, only to be swept away down another street, down another canal. She didn't recognize where she was in the city anymore. But she knew the water was rising. She was only seeing the very tops of the buildings now.

And then, they rose around her and the water began to flow even faster as the dragon rose from the river and the water spilled off his back.

Marielle spilled with it.

Perhaps, if she had been on the mountains, she would have seen him stretch his wings, shake his head and neck and then kick up from the rocks and mud and rise into the air.

Instead, she saw nothing but the corner of a building that cracked into her shoulder and then another that slammed into her leg. And then she was underwater and praying desperately to find the surface again.

It was long minutes until she clawed her way up to the surface and gasped in a long breath. She was no longer on the dragon's back. She'd been swept off and into the river below.

It was even longer until she washed up on a riverbank shrouded in reeds. She pulled herself up on the mud, but she didn't dare rest here. She had to keep moving or she would die.

She told herself that as her head lolled to the ground.

She told herself that as her body refused to move and her eyes closed.

She told herself that as sleep washed over her like the deluge had – just as impossible to fight and just as deadly.

Water always smelled so … alive. It was easy to see why Queen Mer's people revered it. It smelled like life – fecund, thriving life. Even here in the middle of a city that was mostly charcoal, the water was alive.

If Marielle was being honest, the charcoal of the city had been a welcome relief. There was nothing like charcoal to clean the air of scent and her sensitive nose – freshly freed from the clock – was grateful to be able to settle back into constant scenting with a bit of a reprieve.

But at this moment it didn't feel like any relief at all. She could smell the water up ahead, but there was a lot more she was smelling, too.

Fear and desperation pulsed through the air in waves of ginger and acid. The lightning blue of the fear tinging the orange desperation in veins of blue. Her teeth were set on edge immediately, but she couldn't keep her feet from hurrying after it.

She could smell Anglarok in the middle of the street as if he was still there. The smell of insanity weaving through his scent was familiar – Legend. And there were more people scents. At least a dozen. They crisscrossed over and through each other. And they were layered up and over as if some of these people had come here multiple times. Interesting. And a little terrifying.

"Ready yourselves," she breathed, grateful when she heard the sounds of drawn swords behind her. Good. They might need them.

There was the sound of a tiny trickle of water and other sounds – something dull like mud being slapped into place by the handful and the lapping of waves against something wooden.

And everywhere the scent of fear and a scant overtone of smoky red violence. She held her breath as they turned the corner and then sighed with relief when she was hit full-on with the strawberry scent of genius.

"Jhinn!" she called aloud before she'd even seen him, but her eyes found him before anything else.

He was standing with his head tilted slightly as if he was listening to something, but he straightened, wide-eyed at her call. He was in his small boat and his boat was in a fountain pool in the middle of a square. It was large for a fountain pool and the only water Marielle had yet seen – but it was hardly anything to float a gondola on. It was maybe ten times in circumference as the length of the small boat and the edges of the fountain were chipped and broken. It was clear to see that Jhinn was trying to dam it up with debris and mud – but he could only reach what was accessible from leaning outside his small boat.

"You live," he said with a grin as they rounded the corner. Even now, even with despair rolling off him in dark puffs of cloud, even now he smiled. "I knew you would live. I knew this couldn't be the end."

But as he looked around him and up at the constantly moving starry sky, his eyes were full of anxiety. Marielle swallowed. What had she expected? Right now, Jhinn was like a man clutching a barrel in the middle of the ocean with no land in sight.

"It's not the end," Tamerlan said warmly, rushing to where Jhinn was and levering a huge timber up to help shore up a woven wall of sticks and mud.

"It's not full yet, but if I can dam it, then when it rains – if it rains – I can catch water," Jhinn said, laughing as he spoke as if it was the most obvious thing in the world and also as if it were the most ridiculous. "I think it's the only water around. Anglarok came here, but though he watched me like a seagull eyeing a scrap, he only stopped to lap water and then he was gone. Liandari was not far behind, but she was not herself and she barely glanced at me before filling a water skin and then slipping away."

He didn't stop working, even when Tamerlan put a friendly hand on his shoulder. He looked feverish and pale – as if he thought he could work hard enough to keep all the water contained. Marielle watched him carefully. Was he going mad, too, or was he simply a realist? That water in his pool would not last long. Especially if it were the only water source for the whole city.

"The walls need to be high," he said feverishly as he piled more debris on them. "Every time the dragon wheels, a little water sloshes out. If I can just keep it in – just work hard enough to keep it in."

"How can we help?" Tamerlan asked. "Do you need supplies?"

Jhinn shook his head but it kept shaking for too long as if he was hung up on the thought. "Pitch maybe, if you find it. But would that have survived the fire? Wood to heat it. I don't know, I don't know."

He looked up from his work with wild eyes and Marielle could almost sense his thoughts from the scent of fear that permeated them with spikes of electric blue.

"You must be cold," Tamerlan said, offering Jhinn the dark cloak. He had to adjust it over his friend's shoulders and fasten the pin. Jhinn wouldn't stop for long enough to do it himself. And that was why she loved Tamerlan. He thought about whether his friend was cold. He tried to help, even if there was nothing he could do. "Listen. I got you into this mess. I'll get you out."

He made crazy, unkeepable promises.

"You can't get me out," Jhinn said, looking up for a fraction of a second to meet Tamerlan's eyes. "Even if the dragon sets down somewhere, there won't be any guarantee that there is water near. Even if there is water near, I'm in the middle of a city. The canals are empty. There's no way out."

"You could leave the boat," Etienne said, but his tone was obvious – he didn't really believe that Jhinn would leave.

"To leave is death," Jhinn said. "You know that. I couldn't have set a better trap if I'd thought on it for a month."

"How far will you go for your beliefs? For a religion that can't possibly be true?" There was no fire in Etienne's words, though the smell of pity wafted off them.

"It's true, it's true," Jhinn said, balling his hands into fists and hitting them against his forehead. "Even if it drives me mad, it's true."

"Mad?" Tamerlan asked softly, his eyes deep wells of blue compassion. He knew madness if anyone did. Marielle's lip trembled a little at the thought. She could see the confirmation in his eyes – smell it in the elderberry of his scent.

"I swear I saw my brother in the shadows," Jhinn said with an eerie tone. "Is that not madness?"

Marielle leaned on the barrier as she tried to get a better look at his face, but she had to pull her hand away almost immediately. The edge of the pool was slick with a fine coating of ice. It took her a moment to see that the edges of the pool were rimmed with a delicate trim of ice, too. It was getting colder.

If this pond froze over – she'd heard that could happen in cold places – then what would happen to Jhinn?

"Did your brother live in H'yi?" Tamerlan asked.

"My brother has been one of the dead for a very long time," Jhinn said and almost without warning, Tamerlan lunged forward and grabbed him in a sudden hug. Jhinn looked surprised, but he patted Tamerlan's shoulder distractedly.

He pulled back as quickly as it had started. "I'll find a way, Jhinn. I'll get you out of here somehow. And on water. You won't pay with your life for what I did."

"I don't blame you, Tam," he said quietly. It was strange how easily they communicated, as if they could read each other's thoughts. Maybe it was their long months of working together, their similar pasts, their genius minds that worked in opposite but similar ways. "But you should know everything got soaked in the turmoil. I have your spice – what's left of it, but it's soaked through."

Tamerlan nodded. "I have six rolls left."

"Then use them wisely."

"If I find pitch, I'll bring it. What else do you need?"

"I don't dare light a fire. Not in here. Not with the chance of burning my boat. Unless you find a metal brazier. I could use that. A fire would be nice," he said. "And food. If you find any –"

"Of course."

They clasped hands and then Tamerlan turned to Etienne and Marielle. "Food first or do we chase one of the Legends – and if so, which one?"

"Anglarok," Marielle said without even waiting. "He asked for help. Liandari doesn't want help. So, let's go free him."

"I doubt we'll be able to free him," Tamerlan said, looking in the distance, but it was obvious that he wanted to, that he agreed with her that they should at least try.

"We can free him," Etienne said firmly. "Just not in the way we might like. Lead on, Marielle. Show us to your mentor."

Marielle felt her cheeks flushing. If it came to a choice between being an avatar or dying, which would Anglarok choose? It worried her to think that he might not be able to tell them – that they might have to choose for him. She knew what she would choose, what Etienne would choose, what Tamerlan would choose, but her feet felt heavy at the worry that Anglarok might choose differently. Maybe he would rather live- even if it was a life possessed. But if that was true, would he have written the message in his own blood?

A chill swept over her that had nothing to do with the aching cold of the air. This city was haunted by more than the dead of the fire or the ruins of the city's dreams. It was haunted now by those who shouldn't live at all – by the Legends.

Maybe Tamerlan was right. Maybe the Legends really were the true enemy.

4: WINTER COLD

TAMERLAN

Tamerlan's hands shook as he leaned out over the bow of the gondola and strained to see. He'd lost feeling in his feet an hour ago. His fingers were thick with numbness. They'd stopped hurting – which couldn't be a good thing. There was no way to get dry in the gondola and they were all soaked to the skin and wearing soaking wet clothing.

"She's lost to us," Etienne said quietly. He hadn't said that for at least ten minutes – a record amount of time considering how many other times he'd said it over the last hours.

"She's here somewhere," Tamerlan said. "We just have to find her."

"There's a cabin up on the bank in the land of the dead," Jhinn said through chattering teeth. His lips were blue.

Tamerlan had only ever read about cold so intense or about people freezing to death, but the books had all been clear that it was pretty much inevitable if you were this cold and wet.

Forget the girl. We have a greater calling, Ram said in his mind. Tamerlan shook as the Legend tried to wrest control from him again. He'd been doing that ever since the clock was shattered, ever since they plunged off the side of the dragon and into the river below, ever since the dragon flew away.

Marielle had surprised them both with that cunning move. Etienne most of all. And though he'd fought against it, the look in his eyes now was one of pure relief. He was almost too cheerful considering their circumstances. Tamerlan thought that might be why he wasn't fighting hard to stop looking for Marielle. He was a free man. Free in a way that Tamerlan never could be. It wasn't just one Legend in his mind but all of them. And there was no way to destroy every Legend.

"You could find wood in the cabin. Maybe even a brazier. We lost the one Etienne found in the city in that mad flurry over the edge of the dragon. We could dry our clothing and warm ourselves."

"Marielle is here somewhere," Tamerlan said through thick lips. It felt like too much effort to talk when his face was so numb.

"We can't find her if we're dead," Etienne said reasonably.

He was endlessly reasonable now that his mind was his own again.

Tamerlan looked up at the cabin Jhinn was pointing to, but his eyes were so tired. They drifted down as if he couldn't even spare the energy to keep his gaze raised. And as they drifted down, his eyes caught on a heap of something dark in the dead reeds on the shore.

"There," he choked out, pointing to the spot. "There."

Jhinn was already turning the boat. "Etienne will just go up to the cabin and find something to make a fire and then we'll keep looking, okay, Tam? We aren't giving up. We just need a fire."

Tamerlan wasn't listening. His eyes were glued on the heap of cloth. Was that steam rising up from it? Just enough that it might be someone's breath? Did no one else see this?

"Back there!" he yelled and with a long-suffering look, Jhinn pedaled the boat toward where he was pointing.

The second their boat hit the reedy shore he leapt from the bow and ran to the heap of cloth, parting the dead reeds around it. They were heavy with water and clinging ice.

Behind Tamerlan, Etienne cursed. "You couldn't have helped us land the boat, Tamerlan? You had to jump out like a lunatic?"

He parted the last reeds and laid a careful hand on the cloth. Was it?

Marielle!

Breath gusted out of his chest as relief flooded over him. Her hair was frozen to the ground and he had to tug it free before he could flip her over. When he did, a stab of fear shot through him. Her lips were blue, barely a hint of breath was coming from them at all. How long had she lain here in the ice?

At least she was still alive. He lifted her with numb fingers, wrenching her cloak free from where it was frozen to the ground, and clutched her against his chest. Sweet Marielle. She was too fragile – too human – for this insane task she'd set herself, defying Legends and involving herself in the affairs of ancient dragons.

He scrambled up the slope toward the cabin. Was Jhinn right? Would there be the means to make a fire there? He'd burn the walls if he had to. He'd do whatever was needed to keep her breathing.

"Hold on, Marielle," he said through chattering teeth.

He stepped wrong on a numb foot and twisted his ankle, but he couldn't feel it. Couldn't feel anything in his feet. He was lucky his hands were still working – sort of.

By the time he'd scrambled through the rocks and trees and found the cabin, Etienne was there huffing in the cold beside him.

"You've got the luck of the Legends, Tamerlan."

Tamerlan flinched. Whatever the Legends were, they were not lucky.

"If Jhinn hadn't seen that cabin, we wouldn't have stopped, and we would have all frozen to death trying to find her." Typical Etienne with his cold way of thinking.

"You sound lighter," Tamerlan said, reminding the other man of the gratitude and debt he owed Marielle. "Like a burden has been lifted."

Etienne fumbled with the latch on the door. His hands were just as frozen as Tamerlan's

The door fell open and the smell of must spilled out into the world beyond. It was hard to see anything in the dark of the cabin with only the moon to light the way, but Etienne moved into it with confidence. Tamerlan stumbled in behind him, barely biting back a curse as his shin struck a stool inside the dark room.

"Someone must use this seasonally. For fishing, perhaps," Etienne said. There was the sound of him shuffling something around. "They even laid a fire ready. One moment."

Flint struck steel and in the shower of sparks, Tamerlan could see the fireplace and the tinder lighting. Etienne leaned over it, huffing into the lit ball of grass until the flames licked it up and he gently placed it between the kindling in the fireplace. Light flooded the room and Tamerlan stumbled to a small cot on one side of the room. He laid Marielle on it as gently as he could. The blankets smelled of dust and disuse.

"Better strip her clothes off before she soaks those blankets," Etienne advised.

Tamerlan nodded, but his fingers were fat and difficult to work with. He fumbled with her cloak pin, finally loosening it so he could slip the heavy fur from her. He laid it over the back of a chair and placed it by the fire. His own cloak joined it. Neither was much good soaking wet.

Her boots were next. They left a flood of water across the floor.

There was a clatter from the other side of the room and Etienne emerged with a large cast-iron frying pan and a gunny sack.

"No brazier," he said tiredly. "This will have to do."

Marielle's breath was so faint as Tamerlan worked to remove her outer leathers that he was afraid to even jostle her. Were they too late?

He held his breath as his fingers fumbled over buckles and buttons. There was no sign of Abelmeyer's Eye anywhere. It must have been lost when she was swept up by the water.

"I'll bring the pan and tinder to Jhinn," Etienne said. "I'll be back as soon as I can."

Tamerlan didn't answer. He was hesitating over Marielle's leather trousers. Should he remove those? Would she thank him when she woke – if she woke?

"Stop being a landholder prude," Etienne said from the doorway. "She'll freeze to death if you leave her in those wet clothes. Get them off her, stoke up the fire and get yours off, too. The best heat is skin-to-skin. I'll be back with Jhinn's clothing to dry by this fire as soon as I can. We won't be able to make a good fire in this frying pan – not good enough to dry everything."

Tamerlan nodded, waiting for Etienne to leave and shut the door before he went back to work, doing exactly as Etienne had ordered.

He felt numb all over, but best of all, the voices in his head were silent as if they, too, were too frozen to speak. With care, he built the fire up, laying Marielle's leathers around it and then carefully stripping off all but her underthings. Those he left on her with the half-sodden blankets on the bed. It wasn't the best choice, but she should have a semblance of privacy, shouldn't she?

He tried not to look at her smooth skin as he worked. Tried not to think about what it would be like to touch it with fingers that could actually feel instead of these numb icicles.

When he was done, he shrugged off his own clothing, built the fire up even hotter, and blushing like a boy trying to steal his first kiss, he slipped into the cot behind Marielle, shuffled under the blanket with her and wrapped his numb, dead arms around her. If Etienne was right, the skin warmth would help. And if he was wrong and they were still going to die, then this was exactly where he'd want to die. Just like this. With her in his arms.

His arms began to tingle painfully just below the elbows as feeling started to return, but he didn't mind. He let himself savor the moment as Marielle's body went from dead-cold to almost-warm and his own eyelids began to flutter closed as sleep took him.

5: PROMISES MADE

MARIELLE

She woke to heat on her skin and icy coldness at her core. Her eyes flickered open and she drew in a long breath.

For some reason that she couldn't explain she felt so completely safe in this moment. When was the last time she'd really felt safe? Was it back in the Scenter barracks in Jingen? Or was it longer ago than that? Was it at Scenter school? Or further back than that? She couldn't remember. But she embraced this feeling of warmth and safety. Reveling in the luxury of the rare feeling.

Something heavy was over her shoulder and it took her a moment to realize it was an arm – draped over her in the relaxation of sleep. The light hair across the back of it was pale gold like the noonday sun. Tamerlan.

She felt a little thrill stab through her as she breathed in his heady, golden scent, letting it wrap around her consciousness. She shouldn't be doing that. She should be distancing herself from him. Especially since she was planning to deceive him from here on – planning to tell everyone else her secrets and keep him completely in the dark.

And yet she couldn't help it. His scent filled her nose, her mouth, her mind until she was soaking in it. Her limbs moved stiffly as she reluctantly pulled away from his embrace, slipping out from under him. The cold air hit her like a thousand tiny knives but under the moth-eaten wool blanket he was sprawled out in sleep, his mouth half-open and his face almost child-like in innocence. The stubble on his jaw was darker and it softened the hard edges that were starting to form in his boyish face.

She bit back a sigh. In another world – a world without Legends and dragons, maybe she would have met him as an Alchemist's apprentice in the streets of Jingen. Maybe they would have fallen in love – actually, they definitely would have fallen in love – and then she would have married him. And they would be in that bed with a good reason, not just to get warm after an icy near-death experience.

But not now. She pushed back against the memories flooding over her – memories of swirling through the dark waters, memories of Tamerlan breaking down in front of the portal and begging her to stop as she freed the dragons, memories of being in his mind as he battled the Legends.

She loved him. If that's what you called this deep attachment that demanded her complete loyalty and fervent desire to see him well and safe. If that's what you called this obsession that wanted to be near him all the time, to smell him always in the air, to see him smile.

But she was going to lie to him. And that wasn't fair. It wasn't fair to ask him to love her back when she was going to deceive him and break his heart.

With a frown, she crept to where her clothing was hung in front of a raging fire and slipped them on over her dried underthings carefully and quietly. Her skin longed to be back in the bed with his warmth pressed up against her, but the rest of her knew better. Betrayal was best done cold.

Biting her lip, she slipped on her damp boots and cloak, set a few more logs on the fire from a heap of them stacked in an alcove beside the fireplace, and then slipped from the cabin into the world outside.

If Tamerlan was here, then Etienne and Jhinn were probably close by. She needed to find them and they needed to talk. Now. While Tamerlan slept.

There were footprints in the light snow and she followed them down a hill to the river where a pillar of smoke rose up from the small gondola and Etienne and Jhinn – wrapped in threadbare wool blankets – squatted on either side of an iron frying pan filled with a small fire.

She cleared her throat and Etienne looked up.

"You survived the night," he said with a gleam in his eye – but the gleam made her want to sigh with relief. He looked like his old self. "Where is Tamerlan?"

"I left him sleeping." She could feel her cheeks heating at Jhinn's smirk. "I have to talk to you two – without him."

"Without him?" Etienne lifted an eyebrow.

"Without the Legends hearing. Without them knowing. The Grandfather shouldn't be in your head anymore – not now that his avatar is dead. Am I right?"

He nodded, speculation thick in his eyes.

"Then it's finally safe to talk to you," she said, carefully stepping into the gondola. "Jhinn is going to spread the good news to his people on the plains – that they can go to the world beyond the stars and beyond the lands of the dead."

Jhinn nodded soberly.

"But to rid this world of the dragons forever means all of them must go."

"Why do you want to rid the world of dragons?" Etienne asked, one eyebrow lifted.

"You're joking, aren't you?" Marielle asked as she squatted beside the smoky fire with them. "Don't you want a world with no more blood sacrifices? No more fear of a dragon waking and destroying everything? No more Legends coming alive and destroying the innocent?"

"No more magic," Etienne said. "No more power."

She shrugged. "A small price to pay for so much less fear."

He shook his head. "I don't know."

"You don't know?" Fury leaked into her voice. "You were going to kill me to keep the dragon bound and you don't think that's a system that should be stopped? You fought to free me from the clock. You fought to get Jingen grounded again – and now you *don't know?*"

He shrugged and it only made her fury bubble up hotter.

"I like power, Marielle. And I like the world of the Dragonblood Plains."

"And did you like being taken by the Legend? Did you like being his plaything?"

"Of course not."

"Then how else did you see this playing out?"

He shook his head. "I think we go back to the plains and we tell them what we saw and then we let everything go back to normal."

"And the Retribution?"

"We'll deal with them."

"And the ruined cities?"

He let her words hang in the air before countering. "Doesn't your plan involve ruining the rest of them?"

"It involves destroying the avatars of the Legends and freeing the dragons."

"And the ones across the ocean?"

"Those ones as well. All of them, Etienne. There is no other choice. Until the dragons are free, this travesty will go on and on for generations – just as it has been doing. And more innocents will suffer."

He sighed, his gaze going out across the river and up to the waterfall coming down from the mountains. She shuddered at the same time that he did. There were only two options. Neither one was ideal. Both would involve the deaths of innocents. But this was the only way she could see to stop it from going on forever.

"What do you want from me?" he asked heavily.

"Does that mean that you will help me?" she asked, pressing.

He shook his head, rubbing his hand over his forehead wearily. "It means that I won't stop you. But I will keep my people safe, Marielle. As many of them as I can. It's what I was born for, trained for. It's what I'll die for."

She nodded. "That's all I'm asking, Etienne. I'm asking you to go down to the Dragonblood Plains and get the people out of the cities *before* the dragons wake this time. It has to be you. You were Lord Mythos – maybe you still are, I don't know how that works. You are friends with Allegra who has seized Xin. You know how to speak to the Retribution. You can do this. No one else can."

He was quiet for a long time before he spoke. "And you will be slaying Legends. With Tamerlan. Who is going insane hour by hour."

"Yes," she said in a small voice.

"Hoping all the time that he doesn't turn on you and destroy you or make you an avatar, too."

"Yes."

"And how do you plan to do that?"

She looked at Jhinn. "I'm hoping Jhinn will help. We'll need transport. And I need someone else who cares about Tamerlan. Who will help him fight this."

Jhinn was already nodding. "That boy needs help. That's for sure."

"Will you help?" What would she say if they said no? But she could already smell genius flowing off of Jhinn – the smell and color of strawberries. He was thinking. And ambition rolled off of Etienne in russet curls like smoke from the iron frying pan.

"Yes," Jhinn said shortly. "But first, I want my clothes back. Etienne hung them in the cabin to dry."

Marielle was nodding.

"And look for food there. Maybe there's something."

She didn't think there was.

"Etienne?"

He nodded reluctantly. "It will destroy us. Everything will need to be rebuilt from the ground up. The ground won't even be the same."

"It will take the rest of your life," she agreed. He gave her a sharp look and she smelled suspicion. "But at least you'll have a life."

His nod was reluctant.

"We're agreed, then?" she asked. "We can't let Tamerlan know any of this."

"Are you really going to be comfortable lying to him?" Etienne asked. His beautiful features were pinched with concern. She usually forgot that Etienne was beautiful. He wore power and arrogance like a cloak, hiding himself from curious eyes with its protection.

"I'll have to be," Marielle said. The words left a bitter taste in her mouth. She'd just have to learn to be comfortable with it. The fate of the Dragonblood Plains rested on this. "I need to go talk to him."

She was already standing up and stepping from the gondola before Etienne called to her. "You know that for this to work we have to trust you with everything, right?"

"Yes," she said, already striding up the hill.

"I'm not entirely comfortable with that," he said, raising his voice. Anxiety wafted off him, punctuating his words. She smirked as the ochre wafted through the air.

"Get comfortable," she said, not bothering to turn. If she could learn to lie to the man she loved, he could learn to trust her. Saying that over again in her head made her want to snort with the irony of the situation. But it was all they had, and it would have to do.

She was still trying to decide what to say to Tamerlan when she opened the door and snuck back in.

She sat down on the cot beside him, lulled by the warmth of the fire. It was hot enough that she almost wanted to strip out of her clothes – or at least strip down a little. The heat was dry and comforting and if she didn't have a world to save, she would have liked to slumber here all day.

Why couldn't it be like that? Wy couldn't they just have one day of rest? One day to be human for a while?

Tamerlan lay sprawled across the cot, one leg thrust out from beneath the blanket and one arm stretched above his head, for all the world like a gift laid out for her to take. Was there any other way to do this? Could she hide him somewhere? If she did, would the Legends drive him insane or seize him and help him escape? She couldn't risk that. Someone needed to watch him.

Could she leave him with someone else? Not Etienne. He had a job to do. And Jhinn needed to warn his people. Plus, she needed his gondola to get her to where the Legends were. And she needed Tamerlan's knowledge to find them.

No matter how she thought of it, the only way was to bring him with her. Which meant lying to him. She should be shoving him away and telling him that she was a bad choice for him. She should be promising herself not to keep falling more in love with him.

But she wasn't doing any of that. What was the point? Maybe he'd only have a few months left before the Legends took him entirely and there was no Tamerlan left. Maybe only a few days. Couldn't she spend those with him?

She stroked his cheek idly, affectionately. If she'd lived a different life, then all of this could have been different, too …

He pursed his lips as if in a sleepy kiss. One of his hands reached up and found hers, gently drawing it down so that she leaned over him. He kissed her sleepily, murmuring her name. Warmth flooded her – more than just from the fire. Warmth, deep affection and a longing she'd never felt before. It was so sweet it was almost overpowering – and so bitter that it made her ache inside because whatever they had couldn't possibly last. There would be no happily-ever-afters for them.

She kissed him back all the same.

She let herself lose all thought in the tangle of his intoxicating scent. Let him wrap his other arm around her and draw her close, his strong muscles drawing her in so gently that he might have been cupping a baby chick. He murmured her name again – it was sweet on his lips. Sweet as sugar and honey and dreams of peace.

His blue eyes flickered open and a look of surprise filled his face.

"I thought you were a dream," he said in awe.

He had wanted to dream of her. Just the thought made her mouth dry, her heart race, her eyelids flutter. She swallowed and pounced, catching his lips with hers and kissing him more intently than she should, more purposefully than she should.

Gently, oh so gently, he took her shoulders and moved her back so she couldn't reach him with her kisses. She felt her cheeks flare. She'd thought he wanted it.

"I'm …" His words were hesitant. "I don't know if you realize this, Marielle, but I'm losing my mind. Bit by bit."

She nodded, but her eyes were stinging, and she didn't want to hurt him by crying. She tried to blink back tears but hearing it from his own lips made her ache for him.

He bit his lip before he went on as if he was also trying to disguise emotion. "I can't let you ... I can't promise … There's no future in loving a madman."

"Maybe we can stop it." A silly wish. An idle hope.

He nodded vigorously. "Yes, we should stop."

"Not this," she said, half-laughing, half-sobbing. "I meant the madness."

His laugh held no humor but it wasn't scornful either.

"In another lifetime, maybe," he said, echoing her thoughts. "In another lifetime – when I was my own man, I would have asked you in this moment to be my wife. And I would have been so good to you, Marielle. Loyal. Yours to the core. I would have done whatever needed to be done to make a life with you. But now … Like this? I wouldn't give you widow's white for a wedding gift. And that's all I could offer."

She could feel the hot tears spilling over now. Not because he was rejecting her. But because he was so sure he was going to die.

"Please, Marielle, don't cry. Please, sweet Marielle."

And then he was kissing her cheeks, kissing away the tears, his palms on either side of her face, his fingers holding her ears and hair loosely between them. He was always so gentle – so different than the forces that raged within him.

"I won't hurt you. I won't take from you. I will only give."

"What if I want you to take?" she asked, irritated by the weak waver in her voice. "What if I want to offer you strength and loyalty, too? What if I want you to take it?"

"Then I will. I'll never say no to you."

"What if I want the widow's white?"

He pulled his face back, his expression pained at her request, as if she'd slapped him.

Her voice faltered at his expression. "What if I want to marry you, Tamerlan Zi'fen? What if I want the right to know you were mine – if only for a little while?"

What was she thinking? She was crazy. She had just been thinking that it would be better for him without her and now here she was begging for him like a silly schoolgirl. But it seemed almost possible in this glorious hot moment. In the warmth of the fire and the glow of her passion, anything seemed possible. She sucked in more of his scent, intoxicated by it.

He was hesitant. "I told you, I would never say no."

"But would you say yes?"

His lips parted but no words came, and his blue, haunted eyes agreed with the sudden anxiety in his scent. She felt her cheeks heating with the sharpness of rejection.

"Never mind," she pulled away from his grip, turning her face from his.

"Marielle!" He reached for her, his hand resting gently on her arm as if afraid to close his fingers on it.

"No, no of course not. I forgot." She tasted bitterness on her tongue.

"Forgot what?" He sounded confused.

"That you're Tamerlan Zi'fen the son of a landhold and I'm Marielle Valenspear, daughter of Variena the common street whore." Her face felt hotter – so hot that it might burst into its own flames.

"No," he grabbed her hands this time. She tried to pull them away, ashamed, but he held on. "Marielle. Marielle, look at me."

She looked at him, his bright blue gaze almost too much to bear.

"Never that, Marielle. It is I who am unworthy of you. Not the other way around."

She kept his gaze but turned her face as if she could hide while being seen.

"I'm going to have to keep secrets from you because of the Legends. I'm going to have to plan behind your back. I might have to lie to you. I can understand why you don't want to trust me. I don't know why I thought … why I hoped … I'm just a silly girl …"

Her words faded off as he leaned forward, the blanket falling to the cot as he leaned far enough to hold her face again in his hands. The look in his face was so tender, so incredibly soft as if he had made it like that just for her.

"Marry me, Marielle, and claim the right to call me your own for those last few days or weeks I have to give. Lie to me. Work behind my back. Kill me when – eventually – you must. I will never say no to you, only yes. Yes, you may have any part of me you want. All of it, if that is what you want. Every scrap of me left. Every bit of humanity left in me sets to you – like a compass to north, like smoke to the wind – I am tuned to you. Please take what I have left."

She couldn't bear his sweetness anymore. It was too much. She flung herself into his arms, kissing him roughly as if to counter the softness, firmly as if to promise she would keep his scraps safe, determinedly as if to show she would be tenacious at preserving what she could of him, and with abandon as she abandoned hope for her heart.

"Take all my respect and honor, Tamerlan Zi'fen," she said when she pulled back, keeping a hand tangled in his hair. "Take all my love. I will do what is right for you for all my life, honor you, work beside you, fight for you."

And this time it was him kissing her, sealing their promises in the way of their people as he repeated the same vow.

"Take all my respect and honor, Marielle Valenspear. Take all my love. I will do what is right for you for all my life, honor you, work beside you, fight for you."

Marriages in the Dragonblood Plains were serious things. But there was no spectacle. There were only promises said in secret and then the declarations made to family.

And neither of them had family they wanted to declare anything to ever again.

They clung to each other, drinking in the sweetness of this – the one moment they knew they could share – until the fire burned low and Marielle pulled herself from Tamerlan's embrace.

"Jhinn is waiting for his clothes," she said. But she wished she didn't have to say anything. She wished she could spend the rest of her days here in this cabin with him and forget about dragon and Legends and everything else.

But how can you forget your enemies when they are inside the one you love most?

6: Promises Kept

Tamerlan

Etienne and Jhinn were thick as thieves, huddled over a smoldering fire in a frying pan when Tamerlan and Marielle joined them. It was all Tamerlan could do to keep a smile from his face despite everything.

These ones are plotting against us.

He felt his hand twitch and he kept it under firm control. The Legend had nearly taken him up there with Marielle. He'd felt Ram looking for a crack – any crack – even while Tamerlan was confessing his love to Marielle. He'd heard the Legend screaming in his mind that now was the time to pin her hands to the ground with knives even as he'd been kissing her, trying to fight every whisper of violence with added gentleness. He was a monster. He knew that. He adored this woman. He'd married her. And he'd done it all knowing there was a monster inside him who might spring out and destroy her given even the slightest chance.

He must not let that happen. He must never let the Legends get a hold of him again.

"I have your clothes," Marielle spoke from beside him and just the tenor of her voice sent little chills up his spine and little flashes of memory of what they had just said – just done. If he died right now, he couldn't be more happy. The smile dancing in the corner of his mouth was genuine.

He just had to be strong. He just had to keep those Legends back for long enough that Marielle could do whatever she was going to do. He would be complicit in her deceit. He would keep away when she planned. He would let her do as she must. He was utterly, devotedly hers.

If you don't kill her, she will kill you. Surely, you must know that.

She wouldn't kill him unless she had to. If there was anyone he could trust, it was her.

You know nothing. You understand nothing.

He understood – finally – that Ram was his enemy. All the Legends were. At the beginning, he'd thought the enemy was Etienne. And then he'd thought it was the dragons, but now he was beginning to know the truth. The enemy lived inside his mind, breathed his air, thought with him.

We are not your enemy. We are the only ones with the guts to do what we must. We are the only salvation you will ever have.

His hand snaked to his sword grip and the dry wood he was holding fell to the ground. He fought the sudden hold of Ram over his hand, fear spiking through him. What if Ram had wrestled control away an hour ago? What if he had crushed Marielle with his own hand? He needed to be more careful.

He gathered up the wood as Jhinn took the clothing from Marielle.

"Clumsy, Tamerlan?" Etienne said.

Tamerlan looked up. Could Etienne see the guilt in his eye?

As always, Etienne watched him like a hawk watching a mouse. It was hard to know you held a deadly secret with someone like that nearby.

"My apologies," he said mildly, offering the gathered wood to the other man.

"You two certainly took your time," Etienne said, his expression unreadable. "Anything to confess?"

Tamerlan caught Marielle's eye and she blushed. Warmth blossomed in his chest. He made her blush. That was good, right?

"It looks like there is something," Jhinn agreed, stowing away the dry clothing in the hatch of the gondola. He and Etienne were already dry and dressed. Those clothes must have been extra.

"There was no food in the cabin," Marielle said, changing the subject.

Etienne held Tamerlan's gaze until Tamerlan cleared his throat and spoke quietly, "We spoke vows. We declare that we are married."

Etienne's eyes grew wide. It was nice to know he could still be surprised sometimes. "And what, you're telling us instead of your family?"

"You are my family," Tamerlan said looking to Jhinn who the comment was for. Jhinn grinned, a mischievous twinkle in his eyes.

"Well hop in the boat, married man. We have miles to float and I think you should take the first turn at the pedals. It might take some of that spring out of your step."

Etienne looked less pleased, shooting worried glances at Marielle whenever she wasn't looking, and suspicious ones at Tamerlan whenever he *was* looking. But as Tamerlan settled into the seat and began to pedal, he focused inwardly instead of on Etienne. He would need methods to keep the Legends in check.

Good luck with that. I will be recruiting help.

There was no one to recruit.

I think it's obvious that your little love plans to do the same thing to all of us that she just did to the Grandfather. Remember how hard they fought to prevent the extermination of the Legends when it was Grandfather Timeless doing it? They will fight again.

Why wasn't he hearing them, then? Why only Ram.

I have you more fully in my grip. But they will join me now. They will join me when they realize what a monster you have become.

The others spoke in hushed voices, occasionally looking in his direction. But their looks were furtive. Even Marielle's glances at him were hooded, though she also offered secretive smiles that sent tingling sensations through him at the promises they suggested.

He didn't concentrate on their voices. He knew they needed to work without him. Instead, he focused on pedaling the gondola and focusing inward. He imagined that the cast-iron frying pan in the gondola was in his own mind and that every movement of the Legends was being thrown into that frying pan and burned up. He threw his fears in with them. His insecurities. His suspicions.

It won't work. It never does. We will find a way in.

And as the voices of the Legends began to surface again and he could pick them out one by one he focused on the frying pan in his heart, the one full of the flames he would use to burn the thoughts they tried to feed him and the horrible suggestions that they whispered in his ears. It took everything he had to pedal the gondola and to feed the fire. He let both tasks consume him until eventually, Marielle put a hand on his shoulder.

"You've been pedaling all day. We're going to stop up ahead. We think there's a spot where we can build a fire and rest for the night. You need to rest, too … husband."

The word was tentative, but it filled him with a profound sense of joy. He was smiling before he realized it, pulling her toward him for a kiss. But the moment he let the pan fire in his mind slip away, the voices roared through it.

Avatar! Make her join us! Stop her plans. The dragons must be stopped!

They were talking over each other so viciously that he gasped, unable to tell one voice from the next in the cacophony. Marielle misunderstood his gasp, deepening her kiss.

Someone cleared his throat and then she was drawing away, leaving him both aching for her and terrified of what might happen if he let himself go again. Behind his mental steel, the Legends were joining forces to destroy them all.

Snow drifted down as they pulled the gondola to shore and built a fire under a spreading tree. It kept the worst of the snow away, but they still ended up huddled around the fire with nothing in their bellies and no reprieve from the bitter cold.

Tamerlan held Marielle in the growing dark, grateful for the honor of having her in his arms even as the Legends buffeted his mind for control. But it was still a relief when two hours later Etienne declared the camp a "complete disaster" and convinced them to gather wood and go back to the gondola. They fed the fire in the frying pan and Tamerlan took a place at the pedals while the rest of them sprawled out on the boat floor.

"You can't spend all night pedaling when you already spend the day doing it," Marielle said, trying to reason with him. But he was too afraid to listen.

He kissed her chastely but refused to be budged.

Exhaustion was the least of his worries. Legends were far worse than that. And if he let himself cuddle up beside Marielle on the boat floor, he wouldn't be sleeping anyway. What was worse, battling Legends for the salvation of love of his life or pedaling the boat while meditating to keep them at bay? He thought the second option was safer.

They found a village on the second day and Etienne slipped in and bought food from the villagers. There was no inn there and the populace greeted him with suspicion, so they carried on another four days, sleeping in the boat, eating over the frying pan fire. Stopping from time to time to gather wood or slip into the bushes for necessary moments. But they never stopped longer than was absolutely necessary.

And through it all, Tamerlan focused on the pan fire in his mind and threw himself into pedaling until he thought his legs might fall off.

He lost track of the days and nights until the moment that Marielle announced they had reached the plains. Like a spark hitting tinder, the Legends attacked.

One moment, he was in his seat pedaling. The next he was writhing on the floor, his own hand trying to strangle him.

Marielle lunged toward him and he cried out. "Stop! Don't come near!"

His other arm flailed wildly for his sword as his feet kicked at the side of the gondola.

We will have you. Ram.

Quick! Get him on his feet! That was Lila.

Who has the sword? Deathless Pirate.

Marielle was saying something. She sounded panicked, but he couldn't hear her with so many voices in his head.

Now is our chance! Don't let him shake us off!

Ram had done it. He'd rallied the Legends against Tamerlan and all that meditation had done nothing except slow them down. He tried not to panic. He tried to find a way to fight back.

Stop fighting us, pretty man. We have work to do and we'd prefer to keep you in one piece.

The hand on his throat tightened.

And then Etienne yelled something at him – something he couldn't understand. He knew the man was going to attack and he couldn't help but be grateful for friends in a moment like this one.

Something struck him in the head.

Everything went – mercifully – black.

7: Dragonblood Plains

"I worry that you struck him too hard," Marielle said as she bathed Tamerlan's head with a cloth. A lump the size of a goose egg had formed on his head and his beautiful face was lined and twisted despite being unconscious. He muttered under his breath about dragons and avatars.

She swallowed. This was the third day since Etienne had hit him. Three days of fretting. Three days of worrying that when he emerged, he wouldn't be himself anymore.

"It wasn't me who married a madman, Marielle," Etienne said grimly. It was his turn at the pedals. They'd all taken turns at them and though Marielle had wanted to stop at the inn in the last town, she hadn't bothered to voice that desire. She was worried about moving Tamerlan. She was even more worried about what Etienne might do if she left him alone with her brand-new husband.

Etienne had trussed him tightly and tied him to the gondola. And though Jhinn and Marielle shared worried looks as they tended Tamerlan, they agreed to truss him again whenever they were finished.

"We don't know what will surface when he wakes. He might not be Tamerlan anymore," Etienne said harshly.

"We all owe him." Marielle made her words less harsh than she wanted them to be. It would be easy to feel the same as Etienne if she didn't desperately love Tamerlan. Easy to let fear and loathing overwhelm gratitude.

"I owe a lot of people," Etienne said. "And I would kill some of them if I had the chance. Just because someone did one good thing one time doesn't mean they aren't a monster. And monsters must be slain for the sake of society."

"What is society except for a collection of people," Marielle snarled. "And what are people but monsters in clothing and with fine manners?"

Jhinn snorted a laugh at that. He was fishing from the bow as Marielle looked after Tamerlan. He'd already caught two catfish and Marielle's mouth watered at the sight of them flipping on the floor of the boat. Or at least, it did until she remembered how Tamerlan had flipped just like that as the Legends tried to steal his will.

"The Legends don't have him yet. He still has fight in him," Jhinn said, absently. He seemed more interested in the fish.

"The people are more than the sum of individual lives," Etienne said. The closer they got to the plains, the more he took on his arrogant assurance that he was a ruler and not a vagabond like the rest of them. The Vagabond Ruler. That was what history should call him.

Marielle shook her head. "I used to think that, Etienne. I used to care about 'the people' as if that was a thing that trumped individual people. But I don't think that now." She ran her fingers softly down the stubble growing on Tamerlan's face. "Not after being in the clock. Not after opening the portal for the dragons. Not now. Now, I think that individual people matter. That maybe they matter more than 'society' or 'the people.'"

"You're wrong."

It didn't really matter what Etienne thought about that. It only mattered that he saved as many people as he could while she defeated the Legends.

"Now that we can't trust Tamerlan to help us even a little bit, he has become a liability," Etienne said, his voice frosty. "We can't afford to slip up if we want this plan to succeed."

Marielle swallowed. If he tried to hurt Tamerlan, she would have to fight him. And he would win. She knew he was a better fighter than she was, and he was larger, too.

"I've thought about it for the past few days," Etienne said. "And while I don't like this at all, I think you are right that the dragons must be freed. This chain of events that has shaped the cycle of our world for so long must finally end. Do you realize what that will mean?"

"No more sacrifices," Marielle said, turning her eyes to the horizon. "No more innocents sold by their families to die."

His laugh was almost a bark. "And no more temples to Grandfather Timeless. No more 'Queen Mer library'. No more Summernight or Autumngale. All our past traditions, gone. All our rituals over. Do you know how we will devastate the people we are going to 'save.' Do you know what it will take to rebuild?"

"I can't think of that right now. I can only think about the task at hand."

She was surprised when Jhinn spoke. "No more Waverunners, either. You'll have to find new transportation."

"How will your people get up those falls?" Etienne asked wryly.

"Leave that to us." He went back to fishing, his attention completely focused on moving the line just so as he trolled across the bottom of the river.

It was warmer now that they were headed south and east – unseasonably warm. It was as if Spring was coming three months early. Had they disturbed more than the mountains when they set the dragons free? Had they changed the seasons somehow?

"Well, then. No more Waverunners, either. We'll be a people adrift," Etienne said after a moment. He smelled of sharp regret – a scent not unlike red wine – and Marielle frowned at the scent of it. But traditions and temples were not her concern. Justice was her concern. And there would be no justice while the dragons were chained and innocents were slaughtered to keep them bound.

"You'll make new heroes," Marielle said, her voice raw.

"Yes."

"There will be new holidays and new people to venerate."

"Exactly."

She turned at his words. Her brow furrowing. It was as if he was saying more than she understood. She looked a question at him. She could smell something new in his usual mandarin and rust scent. It wasn't quite ambition – but it wasn't quite determination either. It was something in between. Something she hadn't smelled before.

"You can't possibly destroy all the avatars yourself, Marielle. Not with Tamerlan in the condition he's in. You're going to need help."

She sighed the sigh of someone who was barely carrying the burden they already had as someone loaded more on their back.

"Which is why, after much thought, I have decided to help you. Not just to evacuate my people – but to help with everything."

Her eyes widened. "I thought you didn't like this plan."

"I still don't. But I've turned it over and over in my mind and I can't find a better solution. You're headed to Yan first, right? That's where Lila Cherrylocks was said to be buried."

She nodded.

"And I'm headed to Xin to see Allegra," he said. "When I am there, I will go to the sunken island where Deathless Pirate's avatar sleeps and I will dispose of it. I have been there before. I will be able to find it."

She let out a long breath. He was going to help her! She didn't need to do this alone!

"Let's count them out," he said, his dark gaze meeting hers as if they really were a team again. "King Abelmeyer and the Lady Sacrifice are gone with the passing of our friends. Maid Chaos is gone."

"The Grandfather killed Byron Bronzebow and Queen Mer," Marielle said. "And the Smudgers made a new Maid Chaos. And the Retribution made a new avatar in Choan."

She saw a muscle in his cheek flinch at that.

"If I can get to Deathless Pirate and you can find Lila Cherrylocks, then that is two more."

"Do you ..." Marielle hesitated. "Do you know where to look for Lila Cherrylocks?"

He laughed. "She is the worst kept secret in history. Everyone knows – even if they don't know."

"What is the legend?" She let her gaze drift to the shore where snow had all but disappeared leaving fresh shoots coming up in between the dead stalks of grass from the last year. Too soon. It was too soon for Spring. It was as if her life had sped up now that it was almost over.

Now, why had she thought that?

Etienne cleared his throat almost as if he could sense she was distracted. "You tell me. What do the children on the street say about Lila?"

"That she traded her soul for a crown." Marielle's eyes caught on a tree in full flower. The white blossoms shook and battered at each other in the wind so that the ground under the tree was white with them. Just like she would shake the Dragonblood Plains until there was nothing left of them. She swallowed.

"Yes." Etienne's eyes glittered, still focused on silly stories as Marielle tried not to break under the burden she bore.

"That doesn't tell me anything," she said, tearing her eyes away from the tree.

"Doesn't it? They say that she was distilled into a crown. The crown contains her avatar."

"That doesn't make any sense. A grandfather clock – well, someone can be trapped in there, but a crown?"

"And Queen Mer bleeding pearls makes sense? Maid Chaos being reborn into some poor soul makes sense? The magic of dragons is nonsensical because it is not of this world. We saw that in the mountains. It explains so much that always puzzled me. It doesn't follow our rules. It twists and turns as it will."

"Are you saying that the magic of the Legends is stolen from the dragons?"

"Of course."

"So, all magic will be gone when they leave us?"

He gave her a long look. "Do you still think it's worth it to free them?"

"I still think it's necessary."

He nodded.

"But there are many crowns. It will be hard to find the right one."

Etienne snorted. "I doubt that. I heard rumors that Variena was looking for it. Go find your mother, Marielle, and you will find the crown."

Marielle swallowed. The last thing in the world that she wanted was to see Variena again, but if she had Lila Cherrylock's avatar at her disposal, then Marielle had no choice at all, did she?

They sped down the river as it began to narrow, and her mind raced as she tried to think of what she would say to the woman who had sold her life away.

8: CHAOS

The tiny port town flashed in the sunlight as they approached. It was mid-morning and the wind was blowing with them, carrying them down the river so quickly that it was all Jhinn could do to turn the gondola and sneak them into the docks there. Marielle tried to help him with one of the long poles they'd cut to serve in place of oars.

On the docks, fishermen were already returning with the catch of the morning, and for the first time in weeks, Marielle caught sight of family boats with small fires burning, food cooking, laundry being hung on lines across the center of the boats, and children screaming and hopping across the decks. Was Jhinn's childhood like that? She could almost imagine him half the size he was now, leaping and playing like that with Rajit. She began to smile as she glanced at him at the pedals but he shook his head with a knowing frown as if he could read her thoughts.

"I'll find another boat here to take me to Xin," Etienne said abruptly. He was gathering his things. Marielle hoped he had enough coin for that. She hadn't heard a lot of jingling and she knew that she'd already spent what she had in the last village buying food.

She must have looked for too long because when her gaze traveled up again, he quirked an eyebrow. "Are you out of coin?"

"Yes."

He opened his belt pouch. Marielle had thought he might hand her a coin and was ready to thank him but reject it politely. Instead, he pulled out a letter sealed with wax.

"It's a bearer letter. It won't help you until you get to a city, but the banks in any of the five cities will lend to you on my credit."

"What credit would you have now?" She didn't mean to be cruel, but his assets must have been wiped out with the fall of Jingen.

"A name and a reputation of power afford more credit than you might imagine," he said, pressing the letter into her hand.

She stuffed it into her own belt pouch. She didn't have to use it if she found another way, and it would be impolite to deny him.

"Thank you – " She would have said more but a groan from Tamerlan drew her attention. She hurried to his side as he sat up.

"Does your head hurt?" she asked immediately as she helped him sit.

He was staring at his bindings. She reached to loosen them but froze when Etienne and Jhinn both shouted "No!" at the same time.

They shared a glance she couldn't read but anxiety puffed up from Etienne like clouds of smoke in a thick ochre and it rolled off Jhinn like a wave, with fear mixing into the brew like flashes of blue lightning. His eyes were huge as he watched Tamerlan from where he was frozen in place in the boat.

It was Jhinn she looked to for answers.

"I can see her as plain as day," he said. "Lila Cherrylocks."

"You've been up to trouble, little Watch Officer. Haven't you?" the voice was Tamerlan's but the curving smile was not. Nor was the sharp look in his eye. There was none of the gentle tenderness he had for her there – none of the obsessive love that had saved her again and again. This creature was as foreign inside his skin as it would be to see a sheep stand up and ask for roast beef. "Release me and you won't lack for coin. You were just mentioning that you're a little short, weren't you?"

"I thought Ram was controlling him?" Marielle said, looking to Jhinn.

The boy shrugged. "I see him there, too, but someone is holding him back. They're lost in the fog. The ones who don't have him are harder to see."

Superstitious gibberish. And yet it was all true. Marielle shuddered.

"I told you that bindings were necessary," Etienne reminded her, though the look on his face was just as unbelieving of Jhinn as hers must have been. "Don't get soft on me now. Wait here with him and I'll return with food and see if I can book passage to the east."

Their gondola slid into the dock and Marielle wrenched her eyes from Tamerlan long enough to see that the docks were surprisingly crowded. A horde of people had slowly filled them – so silently that she hadn't noticed it while she was distracted. While they had been filled with fishermen and Waverunners before, those people were gone, replaced almost magically by silent crowds of people dressed in muddy rags and holding burning braziers. Smudgers.

Perhaps the regular people had fled. It was certainly her first instinct.

She hadn't seen Smudgers in a long time and their silence was eerie. The gondola bumped against the dock and Jhinn tied it to the brass ring on the side of the dock. His movements were slow, his eyes on the crowd.

Should they run? But the crowd wasn't violent. They were just silent and staring. They even backed up to give Jhinn more room to work and when Etienne – anxiety intensifying around him to the point where she had to pull up her scarf to mask some of that heavy paprika scent – stepped up onto the dock, they cleared a space for him, too.

Something was moving forward from the back of the crowd.

Marielle tried to pick out what it was, but the village was hard to see with so many people crowding in. What had been a bustling market and small flocks and herds on the hills nearby was now just a solid wall of bodies with a small ripple running through it.

Jhinn leaned forward just a little further to cinch his rope tight at the same time that Etienne took a step into the crowd.

And then silently, as if a signal had been given, someone grabbed Jhinn's arm and pulled, tossing him into the crowd like a caught fish. A scream of horror wrenched from him and Marielle had just enough time to gasp, fumbling for Tamerlan's sword. Hands reached out and plucked her from the gondola, dragging her into a mass of bodies.

She screamed at the horror of their silent attack, but the only sounds she heard were the sounds of the wind and the waves, the flocks on the far hills, and her companions screaming, too.

She twisted, trying to fight a dozen hands that held her and dragged her through the crowd. Had they taken Tamerlan, too? Had they unbound him? He wasn't screaming with the rest of them – actually, Etienne and Jhinn had quieted now and all she heard from them were grunts and the sounds of struggle.

It didn't feel real.

But the hands pawing her in smoky silence were real.

And the smell was real, too. She hadn't noticed it at first in all the anxiety of Jhinn and Etienne at Tamerlan's awakening, but here in this crowd was a bubbling, stinking oneness. The Smudgers around her did not smell of normal human emotion – not of petty jealousy or loves and hates, not of rank ambition or bubbling creativity. They all smelled exactly the same – with the exact same dull throb of insanity – astringent and sharp.

But as they moved her through the crowd, the scent intensified until they dropped her on the ground in front of something that stank so strongly of Elderflower insanity that she was surprised she hadn't smelled it from upriver. She'd thought having the wind at their backs this morning was a blessing. Instead, it had left her blind to this.

By the time she squirmed until she could see the source of the stench, she wished she hadn't seen it.

On a platform made of rubble, a huge unlit pyre set behind her, stood a woman with long dirty hair. Chunks of mud clung to strands of it and matted across her scalp and her clothing was stained and torn as if she paid it no attention at all. On her face was a look of pure rapture and when she opened her eyes and looked at Marielle there was nothing but two empty pits staring at her.

The scream began to bubble in Marielle's throat at the same moment that Etienne spun free of his captors, his sword out and slashing. They hadn't disarmed him. Almost as if they hadn't realized he could be deadly at all. Hands dragged Marielle and Jhinn up over the rubble to the feet of the specter that had once been a woman – the specter Marielle recognized as the poor creature who had once been a Smudger and now was the second avatar of Maid Chaos.

There was the sound of something thumping on the ground not far away and she turned to see Tamerlan thrown there, still bound, his eyes shut tight. Beside him, they dumped things from the boat. The cast-iron frying pan. Fishing gear. Blankets. Wooden cups. A few half-empty sacks. A small leather purse that Jhinn kept hidden in the secret compartment of the boat.

Below them, in shocking silence, Etienne battled. He chopped down a half dozen attackers, their blood spraying over the rest of the crowd as they fell in absolute silence except for the gurgling of those unable to breathe through slashed throats and his grunts of effort. Eventually, there were too many attackers. The sword was dragged from his hands and he disappeared under the swarming mass without a sound.

A keening sound filled the air – her own fear slicing through her lips against her will. She couldn't stop it from rippling out of her in waves. She'd seen many horrors by now, but none so horrifying as this.

Around her, the derelict crowd was smiling, their empty eyes and empty scents a poor match for their angelic expressions.

Maid Chaos smiled, too. And then she gestured to the pyre behind her, and the crowd was reaching for Marielle again. She screamed and screamed until her throat was hoarse as they carried her to the pyre. Jhinn's screams echoed her own and the scent of despair mixed with his horror – the only fresh scent in this dead village. She fought, but there were too many hands. She felt Jhinn fighting nearby. But two were not enough against hundreds.

And as they tied her to the pyre and cinched the knots tight, she smelled something brand new.

Fire.

9: Tangled Hope

He was desperate to see and yet Lila had his eyes shut tight while she worked at the bindings.

Almost there. Almost there. That pretty girl of yours should tie better knots.

Was she dead already? He couldn't tell with his eyes shut tight and couldn't do anything about it with Lila controlling his body. He'd woken to her control. Any advantage he'd had before in the meditation state was gone now. He had not a shred of authority over his own body. Maybe he would never have a shred of it again. He shouldn't have let Marielle say vows to him. He shouldn't have said them back.

But it was hard to regret the best – the purest – the most *whole* day of his life. Not when it was the one thing he could hold onto as his life was slowly stolen from him. Still. She was bound now to a pawn of the Legends. And that was a tragedy.

At least I don't want her dead. You can be happy about that. Ram would be fighting to make her an avatar. I don't want that at all. When I'm done getting us free, I'm going to run as far and as fast as I can go. She can live whatever life she can, and I will do the same.

And Tamerlan would never see his wife again. Never glimpse that sweet determined look in her eyes or be swept up in her view of the world – so clean and sharp and fresh when to him it was all so blurry and difficult.

Think of me. I'll be stuck in your body. I'm not sure if you've noticed but I'm very feminine. You're a terrible fit.

Yes, it was Lila who was the victim here. He gave a mental snort. It was hard to keep himself from railing at her mentally, but there was no point in that. It would only leave him hopeless. And it would only slow her down as she fought to free them. Maybe if they were free, he could take back control.

I have you fully now. And the effect will not wear off. Best to be glad it was me and not one of the others. If I was Ram, I would destroy all you loved. If I was Deathless Pirate, I would set up a tinpot dictatorship and debase myself in revelry. If I was the Admiral, I would be the scourge of your people. Be glad you rolled the dice and got Lila. The worst I'll do is steal a few trinkets. And you might even find that you like that.

He doubted it.

He could smell fire. Feel it on his face. Smell it in his nose.

Was that the rest of his spice they were burning?

Not that it matters. You've already sworn not to smoke it anymore.

For all the good it did him.

It turns out that once the path has been trod enough times, we can find it all on our own. Isn't that nice? We can take you against your will and there's nothing you can do about it. Forever.

If only he'd realized sooner. Soon enough to help the Grandfather rather than stop him. Soon enough to destroy them all.

Well, think of it this way, we'll do more with your life than you ever would. You were going to start an orphanage. You married the daughter of a prostitute. What a waste. I will use you to amass wealth like the world has never seen. We will buy and sell cities. We will rule in luxury and comfort all our days. I may even find that I enjoy your company in my mind.

Never!

But before I do, I have a little job to do. I don't want all the Legends killed, but I've never liked the Maid and now she's burning all our stuff.

His eyes shot open at the same time that his hands were free. They grabbed his belt knife so quickly that he wasn't even sure it had happened even though they were his own hands. Lila was sawing through the ropes around his feet, her eyes quickly assessing the situation. They skimmed right over Marielle and Jhinn tied to a burning pyre.

Oh no.

They were going to die!

Panic filled him even as Lila kept looking, assessing, deciding. She was bouncing up to her feet while he was still panicking. She took two steps and snatched up his sword from the heap of things from the gondola that was burning in the pile beside him. He hissed as his hands burned against the hot metal, but she didn't hiss. She didn't even moan. She was plunging his sword into someone's back while he was still reeling from the pain of its burning hilt.

She was cutting through the crowd like a thresher through wheat while he was anxiously trying to catch glimpses of Marielle. The fire wasn't very high yet. Had it licked her flesh or was she whole?

Let's find out!

They'd all turned their backs to him as if he was nothing and now that Lila was slaughtering them, they didn't know. They died in silence, the ones in front of them none the wiser until their turn came. Lila had killed more than twenty of them before the avatar of Maid Chaos noticed and lifted a hand toward them.

She wasn't fast enough.

Lila charged, yelling as she went. She used Tamerlan's shoulders to batter Smudgers out of the way as he went directly for the Maid. In his body, she was dauntless. She was leaping into the circle around Maid Chaos before the crowd could react, her sword streaking toward the Maid like the flame of a dragon.

Maid Chaos flung up an arm to defend herself and the sword struck with the awful green-stick snapping sound of breaking bone. Her arm was cleaved in two, the part of it with the hand attached sailing into the crowd like a piece of split wood.

Tamerlan gagged on bile, but Lila was unaffected. She spun, meeting an attack he didn't realize was there. Hands that had been reaching for him from behind fell like wheat to the reaper and then she was turning back to Maid Chaos.

"I like this sword," she said. "We're definitely keeping it."

The new avatar had a weapon now. She must have grabbed it from someone in the crowd. A fisherman's harpoon flashed in her hand but as grizzly and magical as Maid Chaos might be, she was taken by surprise. She met Lila's bevy of attacks with skill, but she had only one hand.

Lila knocked her harpoon back and then reached in past the other woman's defenses, closing Tamerlan's free hand around the avatar's neck and squeezing so tightly that he thought his finger joints might pop.

"I love the reach of these arms of yours!"

Instead of his fingers breaking, the structure of Maid Chaos's neck crumbled in his fingers like sand. She shuddered, bucking against the sudden destruction of her body. He blocked out her face, seeing, but refusing to acknowledge what he saw. He hadn't asked for this.

Don't want to save your pretty wife from burning to death?

Of course, he did.

Then look.

He looked. He tried not to remember, but he looked and watching that eyeless face die would have driven him mad if he wasn't already insane.

And then it was done, and the avatar was thrown to the floor. It was almost impossible to believe it was him throwing her to the floor. That it was him scrambling up the pyre through the licking flames. They weren't high yet. They hadn't even reached the place where Jhinn was slumped and where Marielle fought at her bonds. But they were growing with every moment. There was no time to spare.

Lila leapt over the flames and up the wood.

Behind Tamerlan, he heard the sound of shuffling feet, but he didn't dare look back at the crowd. Not when Marielle was fighting for her life. He was trying to get a good look at her face when Lila dropped the sword onto the ground and reached for her.

He almost sighed with relief. They were going to free her.

Lila wrapped his hand around Marielle's throat and he just had enough time to register the look of shock and betrayal in Marielle's eyes before he began to squeeze.

No!

The denial roared through him.

Anything but this!

Do not take her life with my hands!

Better than death by fire.

There didn't need to be death at all! He battered against Lila, but she was too strong. He couldn't get through. He couldn't budge her!

As she choked the life out of the one person who *was* life to him, he shoved every ounce of himself against her. This was his body. It belonged to him. It was meant to be filled by him. It was never meant for her.

He knew he didn't have a chance. He knew it was all over now, but he fought, battering against her sense of self. He imagined it was a bridge extending across the spirit world to wherever her soul was meant to be. Mentally, he shoved her across the bridge and cut it in two.

He had his hands back so suddenly that he gasped, pulling them from Marielle's neck like dropping a hot coal. His breath choked in his own throat as Lila fought back

And then he slumped to the ground, blackness taking him over.

At least he hadn't killed Marielle. At least it hadn't been his hands that wrung the life out of her like a fowl for the dinner table. It was cold comfort as he sank into unconsciousness. Cold comfort as he felt the flames rising. They would all die in that inferno now.

10: Arise Vagrant Lord

He moaned, clutching his belly. Too many feet had kicked him and too many hands ripped at him. He was a mass of bruises. The last two fingers on his left hand stomped almost to a pulp. But he was still alive. He tried to mask his cough. His only hope now was silence.

Someone was battling above. He could hear the clash of steel and a wet sound like something made of steel hitting flesh. This silence in these Smudgers was a horrifying thing. He'd always thought the religion was mostly harmless. He'd been wrong. When he remade this society, he would remake it without the Smudgers.

He clenched his teeth and stumbled to his feet, wiping blood out of his eyes. His head was bleeding profusely, but head wounds did that. No point in getting caught up in it. He'd tend it when he could. He swallowed down tendrils of anxiety. No use getting wound up, either. Cold logic was a man's best friend in a time of conflict.

First order of business – Marielle and Jhinn. Where were they? He stood on tiptoe to see over the heads around him. Shockingly, the Smudgers hardly seemed to care or even notice that their victim of moments before was rising.

Ah. Pyres. A horrific way to die.

Whoever this leader of the Smudgers was must be a sadist. Marielle had linked the Smudgers to a new Maid Chaos. He felt his eyes narrowing as the pieces clicked together. This was her work. Perhaps she sensed the aberration in Tamerlan or perhaps they were killing everyone who came through the village. But then why had there been citizens in sight moments before? Besides, it was a short-sighted way to behave.

But then again, people were stupid. That was a given.

So, he'd have to quell her before moving on. He eyed the ground surreptitiously and then reached down to scoop his sword up as inconspicuously as he could. The Smudgers ignored him. Their eyes were on their leader and a figure fighting her. Tamerlan.

Well, at least he was good for something – for now.

Etienne eased himself through the ranks of Smudgers carefully, trying not to draw attention. As long as he moved slowly and silently, they hardly seemed to notice him. A magic perhaps. A geas put on them by Maid Chaos? Or some result of the spices they burned? Either way, he did not like it. No society could thrive while its people walked in darkness.

He wove through their ranks. He could see the pyre and the flames set at the base. He estimated five more minutes before the heat of the smoke began to burn Marielle and Jhinn. Jhinn looked unconscious and though Marielle struggled, the hope for getting free was marginal. He didn't know how long they could survive once the flames hit them, but even devastating burns should be avoided.

He tried not to hurry as he slipped through the crowd. He'd do this without stirring them. He'd be a shadow among shadows. He controlled his breathing carefully.

Almost there.

He was at the base of the pyre when Maid Chaos fell.

Tamerlan was certainly a brutal killer, despite all his denials. Etienne never thought he was as innocent as he pretended, but it was interesting how loyal Jhinn and Marielle were to him. Interesting that he had tangled them in his web of trouble and yet they still wanted more. If Etienne could learn to be like that, he could use it to reign the Dragonblood Plains more effectively. Perhaps he should –

His thoughts cut off as Tamerlan's hands wrapped around Marielle's neck. No!

He scrambled up the platform through the bodies of the Smudgers. Some of them turned vaguely toward him, taking a swing at him or an almost absent-minded kick. But they were uncoordinated and mindless in their efforts. Whatever hold was on them still had them in its grip. He dodged the blows, but it cost him. His left hand was barely working with his fingers broken. His middle ached as he walked and he wheezed against the pain in his lungs. He was more injured than he would like. He made a knot of that in his mind and set it aside. He could do that if he had to – a little trick he'd learned in his youth.

First priority – getting to Tamerlan before he killed Marielle. Etienne needed her. He'd agreed to her plan – agreed so much that it was his plan now, too, and he couldn't succeed in it on his own.

His heart was beating too quickly as he fought his way forward and he tried not to frown with frustration at its limitations. Tried not to grow angry at his gasping lungs. A body was only so strong. And all men were limited. He must accept that and overcome.

He was almost there. He readied his sword for a killing blow as he carefully stepped between the licking flames.

The fire was hot. Sweat broke out across his skin and his fur cloak was aflame before he could prevent it. He snatched at the cloak pin with his broken hand. It was a tense moment before the fur loosened and fell to the wood beneath his feet. He let out a breath and looked up to see Marielle gasping for breath, her face pale as she lolled against the ropes holding her. Tamerlan was on the wood below her, flames licking at his boots and breeches. Jhinn was still unconscious in his bindings.

Priorities. He would cut Marielle free first. She was most important.

He slid his sword into the scabbard and drew his knife, hurrying to slice her bonds. His mind was racing. Would she be able to stand on her own?

The moment the ropes were cut she fell to her knees.

"Up!" he roared. The flames were already licking at the soles of her boots. Dragon's spit!

He rushed to Jhinn, sawing at the ropes. Out of the corner of his eye, he saw Marielle rubbing at her good eye and trying to lift Tamerlan.

"Leave him! Go! Before you burn for your weakness." His words were harsh, but harsh was what she needed. She was worth ten of Tamerlan. Her death would be a terrible waste.

He caught Jhinn as he fell, slapping the boy hard across the face. "Wake up!"

His eyes fluttered open and Etienne picked him up and flung him from the pyre. That would hurt. He might even break a bone, but he wouldn't die. He saw the boy land on a pile of corpses Etienne had cut down only minutes before. Good. They couldn't hurt him.

Now, Marielle. He rushed to her and tried to snatch her up, but she fought at him.

"No! I have to help him." Her voice was thick with emotion.

"Don't be a fool."

Ignoring her battering hands, he lifted her.

"Please, Etienne! Please don't leave him to burn!"

He threw her after Jhinn. He wasn't sure if he could get himself off the pyre. He'd hurt whatever was wrong internally with those foolhardy throws. Deep, visceral pain lashed at him, ripping through his middle. He bit the inside of his cheek and tasted blood, trying to pull in a breath in the smoke and heat. He choked on it, scalding his lungs.

Dragon's blood. He was going to die here.

Tamerlan's eye opened like something from a nightmare and he stood up like a shot, scooped Etienne up and threw him over his shoulder.

A groan escaped with the shuddering pain that rippled through him at the feeling of a shoulder to his belly. They were moving, but he didn't have the strength to lift his head and find out where. He tried to speak, but his words came out as groans.

Dragon's spit! His body was failing.

He could see the appeal of becoming a Legend. Of transcending the binding weakness of a human body and all its limitations. He could understand that completely. If he hadn't been possessed by the Grandfather for that brief time, he might even desire it.

He flinched at every agonizing blow to his belly when Tamerlan took a step. His shoulder was too hard – like a log being driven into Etienne's belly again and again by an angry warrior. There was a pause and then something knocked against his head. He blinked back stars and made out Jhinn's face – his eyes closed. Tamerlan was carrying them both.

Etienne tasted blood when Tamerlan finally sunk down and let him fall to one side, Jhinn to the other. Tamerlan was on all fours wheezing and choking. One side of his face as bright red with patches of white. Badly burned.

They were in the gondola. He could feel the movement of air around him and the whir of the pedals.

"Hurry!" Marielle's words were breathless. "We lost the weapons. We have no way … No! Not that way!"

He wanted to see what she was talking about, but he couldn't lift his head.

He collapsed into the hull and his mind drifted away.

11: CRUSHED AND BROKEN

"It's true. It's all been true!" Jhinn was whispering, his head close to the woman's on the family boat. Her face was shining with rapture – just like all the others had been.

They were three days down the Cerulean River and just outside the locks into Xin City. In those three days, Jhinn had spoken to every boat they could find and every time he did, Marielle felt more and more impatient. They were already headed to the wrong city. They'd passed right by the canals to Choan and since they'd done that, Marielle had felt like she was itching under her skin. She should be in Choan finding the crown and destroying Lila.

Instead, they were on their way to Xin to find Allegra. But what choice did she have? With both Tamerlan and Etienne grievously injured, they needed a good healer. And the last time they'd seen Choan it was in complete chaos. Worse, they would need money to pay a healer and they didn't have money – except for this bearer note of Etienne's. Everything Jhinn owned had been stolen and burned by the followers of Maid Chaos – the Smudgers.

Marielle paused in pedaling the boat to shiver at the memory. The Smudgers had just stood there, wandering around in circles and looking off into the distance mindlessly as they'd fled in the gondola. In the panic of the moment, she'd barely noticed them as she worked to batter their boats to the side so that Jhinn could pedal them back out into the Cerulean river. She'd had to throw water over him to get him conscious enough to do that.

Even then, Jhinn had wheezed and coughed for hours afterward, muttering, "My feet never touched the land. Not once. They never touched."

 Then she'd tried to tend to Etienne and Tamerlan, binding visible wounds and making them as comfortable as possible in the bottom of a boat.

But the eyes of the Smudgers haunted her now – as did the memory of Tamerlan's beautiful eyes so cruel and distant as he choked the life out of her.

She swallowed, her throat aching and painful.

Despite her best efforts, Etienne and Tamerlan were in bad shape. They both drifted in and out of scant consciousness and it was all she and Jhinn had been able to do to get water or weak broth into their delirious mouths. Etienne's torso was a mass of purple bruises, his face and hands also battered. He'd been nearly trampled to death. That he'd been able to cut them free at all was a miracle. No, it was the result of his enormous determination. She *would* get him to Allegra and repay him for his efforts. She would find a way to get him healed.

And Tamerlan – half the flesh of his face was wet with deep burns. His already blind eye was burned so badly that it made her stomach turn and heave just to look at it. She'd tried to apply wet cloths to the burns to keep them moist – that was what you did, right? But it wasn't helping, and his moans of pain were heartrending.

Her own throat was healing, though her voice was still hoarse, and her neck bruised. She tried not to think too deeply about that. Tried not to remember those moments when she thought the man she loved most dearly might drain the life from her. But the memories still surfaced every time she closed her eyes.

If it hadn't been for Jhinn, they wouldn't have made it to Xin. Each family boat he spoke to, gave him a gift – fresh water, a blanket, food. One even gave him a brazier for a fire. It had been just enough to keep them alive these last three days. Just enough to reach Xin.

And each of those family boats had immediately headed upriver. Jhinn hadn't been wrong. The Waverunners saw his news as the culmination of their beliefs and none of them wanted to be left behind.

"We'll find a way," they always said as they left. "We'll get there somehow."

She wished she could be so confident. Her own task was looking more impossible by the moment.

The family boat headed off and Jhinn smiled at her from the bow. He was holding an oar – a gift from the boat for his news. She smiled back, her exhaustion plain on her face. They'd both been working hard with little sleep – moving the boat, tending the injured, and just trying to keep everyone alive.

And now that they were at Xin, what were they going to do? She was sure that Allegra would help – for a price – but could Marielle get to her?

Marielle sighed tiredly as they reached the city gates. The guards there were stopping each boat and checking it. There weren't many at this time of day. Fishermen went out and came in at dawn and dusk and trading boats were often on the same schedule. Mid-afternoon was much sleepier.

Marielle looked up at the city that rose in the stone island. The last time she'd been here a dragon had just attacked. But that was months ago, and now the city was well on its way to being fully rebuilt. She could see the gleaming fresh stone and wood rising above her. She felt her cheeks heat as she realized that she was going to ask these people to do that all over again.

What was it like to rebuild your life from ashes?

Could she live long enough to find out?

It was their turn to be searched. The guard's tabard was a different color than the last time she had been here. It was pure white with no crest sewn on it.

"Stand and be questioned by the guard of Xin City," he said.

Marielle stood up and he rolled his eyes. Apparently, 'stand' had been figurative. Jhinn held them in place beside the jutting pier with his brand new oar. Only boats allowed past this point would be let up into the city via the lock system.

"Names?" the guard asked. Beside him, another guard in the same white tabard sat at a small wood desk with a pen dipped and ready to write.

"Marielle Valenspear," Marielle said. "I am here with Jhinn of the Waverunners, Tamerlan Zi'fen," that led to a shared look between the guards, "and Etienne Velendark."

The look of shock on their face was so sudden that Marielle didn't have time to flinch before the closest guard had leapt into her boat.

"By order of Allegra Spellspinner, Lady Saga of Xin, Etienne Velendark is to be brought to her immediately." He looked down at Tamerlan and Etienne where they lay with fever sweat on their brows. "And alive."

"That's the plan," Marielle said drily.

"We have strict orders to escort him and any other with him to the palace immediately upon his arrival."

She knew Allegra was fond of Etienne, but she had no idea that the woman was this in love with him. She could feel her eyebrows rising as the guard continued.

"The quickest way will be via this gondola. Is it fit to float as far as the palace?"

Jhinn's snort was insult mixed with fury but Marielle held up a calming hand. "Of course, honored guardian. Please let us float there immediately."

That seemed to mollify him, but it didn't keep Marielle's heart from racing every time he stole a glance at her sleeping husband and friend. He looked at them often – whenever he wasn't ordering the locks to close or open immediately. And his frown deepened as the minutes dragged on.

"Which one is the Lord Mythos?" he asked eventually and when Marielle pointed to Etienne the man nodded grimly.

Jhinn switched places with Marielle at the pedals. He was fresher than she was anyway, his face less lined with worry. And no wonder. His people would be free soon. But she bore the weight of Tamerlan's future and the destruction of her world to save it. And whatever she did, she didn't dare admit any of that to Allegra.

When they reached the palace, her hands were trembling. She still hadn't worked out what to say. How did you say, "I've brought you the lover who chose my fate over your ambitions and incidentally, can you move your entire population so I can destroy your city?"

Maybe you just said it.

She steeled herself for trouble.

The guard spoke to the palace guards and before she could blink, they were floating inside the palace walls to a private landing.

"I'll stay with the boat," Jhinn said.

Marielle offered him a grimace – the closest she could get to a smile.

The guard with them was already speaking to more palace staff and within minutes servants were running in every direction. Whatever happened next was going to determine whether she succeeded or failed. It was hard not to be worried about that.

Instead, she turned her attention to Etienne and Tamerlan, checking their breathing. They were still alive. Still feverish. Still in a lot of pain. Worry tangled in her belly, weighing as heavily as a stone would.

"Marielle." The voice that greeted her was cold but Allegra's lingering scent of traces of vanilla magic and various herbs filled the air.

She straightened so fast that she knew she looked guilty of something and Allegra's eyebrow rose. She was flanked by a ring of guards and even more servants. But, surprisingly, she was dressed nearly identically to the last time Marielle had seen her. She had not donned the elaborate dresses and hairstyles of the Landholds or rulers of the cities and while she wasn't wearing an apron, she was wearing a high-necked charcoal grey dress with tiny grey pinstripes in the fabric. It was serviceable enough to run a shop and cut to compliment her figure, but certainly not what you would expect the ruler of a city to wear.

Marielle tried a curtsy and Allegra frowned, waving it off with a chopping motion of her hand.

"Where is he?"

He could only mean one person. Marielle stood back so that she could see Etienne lying on the threadbare blanket at the bottom of the gondola.

Allegra was in the boat as quickly as the guard had been before her.

"How long?"

"Three days."

She clucked her tongue. "Internal bleeding. Fever. You've almost killed him, you stupid girl."

Marielle bit her tongue against a retort. This tone meant Allegra would help, and that's what they needed right now.

"Bear him to the rooms attached to mine. I will tend him myself," she ordered her guards.

Marielle kept a blank look on her face as she watched the servants and guards lift Etienne carefully onto a litter as Allegra hovered over him like a hen with one chick.

"And Tamerlan?" Marielle asked. "Would you tend him, too? For Etienne's sake?"

She held her breath.

Allegra's gaze was blazing when she turned it on Marielle. "That one is trouble. And I can ill afford trouble at this time."

"Please."

A muscle twitched in her jaw. "You can take him to Spellspinner's Cures. I'll send Fanwen with you and she will tell my people to tend him there."

"Thank you."

"Don't thank me. This settles the debt I owe you for returning the Lord Mythos to me. After this, we are free and clear."

She left the gondola, striding after the litter as her maid – Fanwen – boarded the little craft.

"Allegra!" Marielle called.

Everyone froze and Allegra spun. Her sharp features deadly in the low light of the pier.

"You dare call me by name? Don't be fooled by my simple clothing. This city is mine now."

"My apologies," Marielle said, swallowing. She still needed to say this. Etienne might not recover in time to warn her – might not recover at all. "You must evacuate your city."

"Must?" There was an edge of warning to her voice.

"The dragon beneath it will rise."

"When?"

How long did she dare wait before destroying Deathless Pirate's avatar now? It would have to be her. Etienne could not in his current state. How long would it take to get Tamerlan stabilized? The words froze in her mouth.

"Three days."

Her mouth nearly fell open at Jhinn's words. But he had saved her from struggling with an answer.

"That's not enough time. Certainly not for Etienne, but not for my city, either," Allegra said.

He shrugged as if he and Marielle would have nothing to do with this turn of events. He was right to play it this way. If anyone knew they were going to cause it, they'd kill them faster than an arrow could fly.

"Then you'd best hurry," Jhinn said shortly.

"Three days?" Marielle mouthed, wide-eyed as they pushed out from the pier. Jhinn merely shrugged grimly.

He was right. There was no time to lose.

She'd already seen how the Legends could fight back.

12: Never Say No

MARIELLE

She woke with a start. It was still night.

Whatever Allegra's women had put on Tamerlan's face was almost magical. He had fallen to sleep – a deep sleep, not a fever sleep – as soon as the salve was applied. The relief it brought Marielle was just as tangible.

"He won't see from the eye again," the assistant had warned her. "But the salve is one of Allegra's. They don't call her 'Spellspinner' for nothing. His face will heal. And quickly."

She'd bathed him with a cloth and raided Allegra's storeroom for fresh clothing for them. Allegra wouldn't be able to move it all in three days, so it hardly felt like stealing, and her shop workers did not stop Marielle. Allegra's clothing were dark and cut with sharp lines, but Marielle found a leather vest to go over them and a warm cloak.

Jhinn was off to spread his good news and she needed sleep, but she took the time she could to strip out of her filthy, burned rags and strip Tamerlan out of his. She locked the door of his room and slid under the blankets with him to keep him warm, trying her best not to touch his burned face or the other old wounds she'd tended and bound. It was all she could do.

And she tried not to shiver too badly as she fell asleep, when her mind kept conjuring up the look in his eyes as he tried to kill her. She wrapped her arms around him, as if she could fend off the Legends by guarding him with her body, as if by drawing him closer physically, she could bring back her sweet Tamerlan and expel the demons that held him under their thumbs.

And now that she was awake she looked at his sleeping face in the moonlight as it lit the tiny room in silver light. He looked so innocent, so vulnerable.

His skin was already healing. The assistant had not been wrong about the power of Allegra's magic. Was it drawn from the dragon Xin? His burns were no longer seeping. The skin seemed to be knitting itself back together before her eyes.

She swallowed back a lump in her throat as his good eye flickered open. The one that had been burned was always open now. Even though the salve had sealed shut the open wounds on it, the eye was a bubbled mass of damage. He would need a patch for it. She would be sure to get him one.

"You live," he gasped, relief thick in his voice.

She waited, tense. Was it Tamerlan or was it a Legend in his body?

He coughed. His words were faint. "I fought her off, but I wasn't sure. I couldn't tell if she had already taken your life. Dragon's blood, Marielle. Why are you still here?"

She let out the breath she was holding, relaxing into him. It was him! It was him.

"Tamerlan!" she cupped the undamaged side of his face with a hand. "Oh, thank the Le – I'm so glad it's you."

"You shouldn't be here, Marielle. You need to run," he said, his lip trembling as he spoke. "Flee. Before they get you. They want you dead."

She shivered, but she held her ground. "No."

"Aren't you afraid of me?"

"It wasn't you. It was them."

"I almost killed you with my own hands. I couldn't stop them. I'm not asking you to forgive me." He curled over himself, shaking with anguished coughs. "I don't expect that. The only thing I can do is beg you to leave me while you can."

"And what will you do?"

"Go as far from people as I can go. Keep myself from being able to harm anyone."

It made sense. It really did. And yet she knew she would never want that. Not even with the constant risk that he might turn in her hand like a faulty blade and destroy her.

"No, Tamerlan," she leaned in close so that her dark hair fell over him, her body almost grazing his. She kissed the undamaged side of his jaw, her lips meeting the short beard still growing there. She should have trimmed it. Her kisses trailed up to his cheekbone to slide over the silky skin of cheek and temple, eyelid and forehead. "I married you because I want every moment that you are *you* to be with me."

"I can't let you, Marielle." He sounded like he was breaking.

"You think you can determine my course?" she let a dangerous edge into her voice.

"No, but I *must* determine my own. And my course must not include your needless death."

"Even if I was not laying my heart before you like a Springhatch egg and begging you to take it, we still need you," she whispered into his ear, letting her lips trace the shell of it with a kiss. There might not be many more of these kisses. There might not be any. She should savor them while she could. "You are our connection to the Legends. Without you, we will not know when – " she bit off the word. She couldn't tell him her goal. Didn't dare. "We won't know what we must know. Please trust me on that."

"And Jhinn?" he asked, his voice still wavering.

"Is out spreading the good news to any Waverunner who will listen."

"And Etienne?"

"Will heal. I delivered him to Allegra who seemed more than pleased to take possession of him."

"And you?"

"Am no worse for wear but am entirely sick with love." She felt her face flushing at the admission. But if she didn't admit it now, when would she? If she didn't take every single moment to convince him of her love, she would lose her chance.

She pulled his blanket down lightly and kissed his collarbone.

"Marielle," he groaned. A warning, but not a 'no.'

She let her lips drift to his shoulder, his bicep, press into the hollow of his elbow and the center of his palm.

"You should not."

"I should not kiss my husband?" she teased.

"You should not care so little for your own life that you risk it by being near to me."

He was right. And he was wrong. Because she was beginning to realize that he *was* her life. Every moment with him was life. Every moment without would be a kind of death. She would no more embrace that death than she would embrace the other kind. Not even if he asked her to.

"Do you remember when you told me that you were done saying no to me?"

"Yes," he gasped and she buried her face into the hollow of his neck, kissing it gently.

"Then do what you promised, please."

He moaned at her words, but he did not say no. Not for the rest of the night.

13: To Know and Not Know

TAMERLAN

Tamerlan adjusted the eyepatch Marielle had given him that morning. It rubbed on his healing skin uncomfortably, but shockingly, that healing skin only stung now rather than causing waves of agony every time the wind so much as stroked it.

He tried not to blush at the word 'stroke' in his mind. Marielle had done things last night that had taken a lot of the sting of his wounds from his mind. Affectionate things that he had thought he would never experience now that he was a madman.

The last three days with her, healing as she collected supplies and raided Allegra's storehouses, had been like a kind of heaven. A heaven with one eye and a face he didn't dare look in a mirror to see, but as much heaven as a madman could handle.

And all the while, the Legends had poisoned the happiest moments of his life – the most intense joy and attachment he felt at the nearness and affection of Marielle – with their constant suspicions and whisperings. They did not like her. They did not trust her. And they hoped to poison Tamerlan against the one good person he knew.

To his relief, his body had stayed his own. Whatever control he had wrested from Lila Cherrylocks was still there – for now. Still present enough to keep them at bay.

For now. You cannot be strong forever.

Which was what he was afraid of. He'd tried again that morning to reason with Marielle as they dressed and fled Spellspinner's Cures but she had not heeded him in the slightest. He should have tried harder.

 Guilt shuddered through him at the thought, because he knew he had not fought very hard to make her leave. Not when staying with her was so entrancing. She bewitched him, it was true. Not like a predator playing with prey, but like the rays of light cast from the facets of a diamond, like the colors of the sunrise staining the sky, like the flight of birds over the dark mountains of the north. She bewitched him with beauty so sharp that it shattered his heart and left him gasping.

Your romanticism is hopelessly naïve. It will be your undoing. Can you not see with your eyes what is right before you? This woman will kill you.

She is already preparing you for slaughter. Why do you think she keeps you so close? When the time comes for her to steal your life, she wants you to be at hand.

Liars. They were all liars all the time.

But were they? It was impossible to believe that anyone could love him. Could adore him.

Was the only explanation the obvious – that it wasn't real?

He blinked and swallowed down bile.

He hated it when he wasn't sure if his thoughts were his own. One tiny drift into daydream. One slip of the mind and there were thoughts waiting to colonize him, to enslave him, to ruin him forever.

He adjusted the eyepatch again and frowned at the irony. They had nearly reached Dragon's Spit Point. He was rowing while Jhinn pedaled and Marielle prepared the things she had brought with her. He hadn't asked why they were going there, and he was trying very hard to think of anything else he could. He'd gone through many of his childhood memories all over again just to keep their location from his mind. One slip and the Legends would know everything he did.

Marielle and Jhinn hadn't discussed what they were going to do at all. They'd simply nodded to each other as they wove through the surging crowds of troubled people and seemed to know without words what was coming next.

Maybe they had discussed it while he was healing. Maybe they had discussed it in the hours that Marielle had slipped away preparing. Maybe they were just so in tune with the same plan that they were following it without having to speak a word.

He swallowed. Think about other things, Tamerlan. What would his father be doing in Yan? Had he survived the revolution there? Was he in power now? Would Tamerlan see him before the Legends finished stealing his mind? If he did, what would he say?

He thought of everything and nothing as they crested the waves of the sea, keeping his mind busy so it would not drift to the task at hand.

But it was hard not to think about where they were when Jhinn settled the gondola on a small spit of land – the Bare Island – made entirely of sand.

There was a scream of recognition in his mind.

"Do I need to bind your hands?" Marielle asked gently, catching his eye.

He stiffened at the sudden clamor in his mind, his hands drawing to his temples.

"Please," he gasped, fighting an onslaught from Deathless Pirate.

My island! My treasure! Mine!

"Please, do it quickly."

He'd thought it would only be his hands, but Marielle and Jhinn laid him in the sand, tying both feet and hands with a length of rope behind him stretching between the two. It would be impossible to escape this. Which was perfect.

"Are you sure we should do it this way?" Marielle asked Jhinn, worry on her face. It was the first time they had consulted aloud all morning. "If we die in the attempt, he will lie here unable to help himself."

"Then we don't die," Jhinn snapped. "Wait patiently here, Tamerlan. We will be back before the tide swallows the island."

"Swallows the – " Marielle sounded panicked.

"Don't worry, Marielle," Tamerlan said, making his voice tender as the Legends in his mind began to howl.

They will rob me! They will take what's mine!

"You're making the right choice," he assured her.

She gave him a tremulous smile and then she and Jhinn got back into the boat and began to paddle out to a point just off the edge of the island.

No! Not that! Deathless Pirate's voice took on a new tone and then suddenly it was overwhelmed by Ram's voice snarling in the background.

This was their plan? They mean to slaughter Deathless Pirate's avatar? They will destroy us one by one and the world will burn! You must stop them! You must!

They seized hold of him and shook him and he prayed the knots would hold, that the rope was strong enough as his muscles tensed and bucked, and his eyepatch dislodged, sliding down his face, as they dragged the uninjured side of his face across the sand.

He lifted his face from the sand to peek at Marielle and Jhinn.

In the distance, he could see Jhinn lighting an underwater lamp and fixing it to a chain suspended from his belt. He carried a rope in one hand and a hammer in the other.

Marielle cast an anxious look in Tamerlan's direction.

I will not be laid waste! Deathless Pirate's roar in his mind silenced all thought.

This was why the entire city was departing today. This was why Marielle had refused to discuss the strangeness of people loading everything they owned on mules or in carts, in gondolas or barges, and fleeing for the past three days until this morning half the city had been gone. This was why the guards had tense looks in their eyes. Why the banner had disappeared from over the palace. Why there had not been a ship in harbor when they left. And not a single family boat in any canal. This was why he had asked no questions of her and refused to pay any mind to where Etienne might be.

Because though he wouldn't admit it even to himself until this moment, he had known exactly what her plan would be. She was going to kill every Legend one by one.

And what will she do when she gets to the last of us in your mind, hmmm? Ram's voice was bitter. *When she has reduced our people to refugees and our land to desolation?*

Then she would kill that avatar, too.

Think again, pretty boy, Lila whispered. *We certainly have. We can't all occupy you at one, but once there are no other Legends to vie for your attention, one can easily occupy you. Remember how King Abelmeyer held the girl from over the sea? Remember how the Lady Sacrifice laid waste to her consort? That will be you. If she succeeds, whichever of us lives last will make you our avatar. Roll the dice, watch them spin, which of us will your soul win?*

He shuddered, but now the other Legends were whispering the same grisly rhyme in his mind.

Roll the dice,

Let them spin,

Which of us will,

Your soul win?

They went on with that horrible chant while Deathless Pirate wailed in the background.

Could they even destroy his avatar with a hammer? Marielle had needed to use the Eye last time.

Because the clock was different. The other avatars are not so immune. Remember Maid Chaos? Remember Queen Mer? They are vulnerable. We are vulnerable.

Tamerlan tried to focus his one eye on Marielle anchoring the boat to something. On Jhinn slipping down the rope into the water. On Marielle waiting, waiting, waiting, her eyes drifting to Tamerlan and then to the rope and then back to Tamerlan and then eventually stripping off her clothing and diving in, too.

Sweat dripped into his single eye when they didn't come up. He blinked again and again.

He knew they'd succeeded when across the ocean waves, he saw the dragon crawl out of the stone, flinging rock around it in every direction and leaping into the sky, the city of Xin still encrusted on its back like barnacles.

Deathless Pirate was no longer screaming.

The chant ended in his mind.

We will try another way. You can't defend against everything.

And then silence reigned. But it was not the silence of relief. It was the silence of creeping darkness and waiting terror.

He thrashed against his bonds, worried about his wife and his friend deep beneath the sea. Had they died in their attempt? Had he lost them both?

The ropes cut deeper.

He could not drag his gaze from the gondola.

And then a head surfaced, and he let out a breath.

But his heart froze like a stone when he saw it was Jhinn. Where was Marielle? Where?

Jhinn pulled her, limp and water-logged up into the boat.

No! No, no, no!

He thrashed until he thought he might break his own arms, but he could not free himself. He could only watch helplessly as

Jhinn worked over her lifeless body and pray, hope … moan in anguish.

If she was gone, he wanted nothing more than to be left here to drown on this sand-spit of an island.

He thought he might be crying. It hardly mattered, though it meant that sand was sticking to his cheek.

Jhinn slumped and his heart broke.

No.

He'd given up.

She must be gone.

And he hoped his end would come quickly.

Because now it could only bring relief. Relief from sorrows and heartaches too great for him to bear.

Jhinn paddled the boat toward the sand and beached it, but he couldn't get out.

"Tamerlan?" he called.

Tamerlan tried to answer, but he choked on his own words. Despair was too thick to breathe around, much less speak around.

"Can you roll over here so I can untie you?"

To what end? For what purpose?

"We freed the dragon," Jhinn continued.

At what cost?

"Marielle breathed in some water, but I think she'll be fine," his friend said.

Tamerlan's eye widened. Joy – sharp and painful – squeezed his chest.

"I just don't know if she'll be able to pull herself together and come and get you before the tide rises too high."

Tamerlan squeezed his core muscles to lift his head higher. The island was smaller. And it grew smaller with every movement. The tide was coming in.

He closed his good eye, pinched his lips tightly together and rolled as hard and fast as he could toward the gondola. Hands caught him just before he struck the sea.

"Here we go. Now, don't kill us when I cut you loose, okay? That's a good boy."

He was crying again, but this time it was with hysterical relief.

14: EXODUS

ETIENNE

The track of ground north of the river was worn from so many feet trudging over it hour after hour – and still, people were pouring across it, heading north and west with a grim determination and simmering anger in their eyes.

"They will not forgive me this lightly," Allegra said in a taut voice from her place on the chestnut horse she'd chosen.

Etienne wondered if she'd ever sat a horse before. His own life had provided very few opportunities to practice and it was all he could do to keep the jostling of the creature's spine from stabbing him with shooting pains every time it moved. He already hated the horse. Perhaps he wouldn't have hated it in other circumstances, but three days had not been enough time to heal all his internal injuries – not even with Allegra's near-magical cures and generous hospitality. At least his fingers were healed. He flexed his left hand, testing them again.

She sidled her horse over to his and spoke quietly. Even the twenty guards ringing them wouldn't be able to hear her low tone.

"If your little friend proves fallible and the dragon does not rise, then I will be the most foolish ruler to have ever held Xin."

He still wasn't sure how she'd become the sole ruler of the city. He'd thought she was leading a movement – a group of influential merchants, Landholds and guild leaders at its head. But when he'd awoken to her ministrations, he discovered that it was only her left.

Perhaps the others had died taking the city.

But he rather suspected otherwise.

He suspected that when he began to dig – and he would dig eventually – he would find that Allegra had done what was needed to remove them from contention. And what he hated most was how much that very ruthlessness drew him to her.

After all, it was illogical to side with someone who saw competition as a threat and who dealt with threats in only one way – murder. Especially, since he was most certainly competition.

"And how will the people regard you when the dragon does rise and most of them are safe with you on the far bank of the river rather than tumbling from his back like drops of water from the back of a duck in flight?"

"They will regard me as foolish, still," she said tensely. "Because they will have nothing to rebuild with but what they could carry on their backs and in their carts – not close to enough. Who could have predicted that almost all the boats would leave just before we had news of this need?"

Etienne clenched his jaw. If only he had been lucid, he would have arranged this differently. He would have kept Jhinn quiet until after the evacuation. The loss of all the Waverunners had delayed them by hours they didn't have. And he would have found a way to mobilize Allegra *immediately*. She hadn't believed Marielle's warning until she'd heard it confirmed from his own lips. It was poorly done.

And it was frustrating when he realized he was cut off from Marielle and Tamerlan and now he would have no way to know what they would do next or how they would do it.

Frustrating – but not impossible. He shifted in his saddle. Challenges were a good thing. Why not enjoy them when they came? Maybe if he turned his mind to their goals –

"Riders!" a guardsman said breathlessly, riding up awkwardly on his horse. Did none of them know how to ride the beasts? Then why own them at all?

"From where?" Allegra asked. Her voice held the ring of command. He liked that, too. It was hard to deny how power drew him. The power of the dragon Xin called to him from under the rock where it slept and the power of Allegra sang to him also, each in its own way.

"Choan," the guard said. "They are dressed as Queen Mer's Retribution. At least a hundred of them. On horseback."

How odd. The people of the ships rode as awkwardly as the people of the cities. He snorted at the sight.

He let his gaze flit to Xin. The dragon still lay dormant. People were still fleeing the city. It took time to mobilize thousands into fleeing for their lives. Time to clear traffic jams and more to convince stragglers to actually go. They'd been at it for ages already, and Allegra said Marielle had told her three days. Three days ended this morning and it was nearly noon. How much longer would it take for them to dive down and dispose of the Pirate's avatar? He pushed back a shiver at his own memory of diving down into Deathless Pirate's lair. He'd prefer to avoid that again, though he'd volunteered for the honor before he was injured.

"They wave a flag of parley," the guard was saying. "What should we do?"

"Parley with them, obviously," Allegra said, her gaze running over Etienne like she was wondering what price he would fetch.

"What is on your mind, Lady Saga?" he asked, raising a single eyebrow. The best way to deal with Allegra was to show no weakness.

"I thought that perhaps you would make a good ambassador for us."

"Ambassador?" He could barely sit a horse, never mind negotiate. The pain shooting through his abdomen left him nearly crippled.

"After all, I first met you when you were an ambassador to Xin. Perhaps you have skill we could use."

He nodded his agreement. He would have preferred *ruler*. But he could be *ambassador* if that was what suited best.

He squeezed his horse with his knees the way he'd read that riders did in books, but the creature remained still.

"That one moves when you click your tongue, Lord Mythos," one of the guards said in a low tone.

That earned him an angry scowl from Allegra. Interesting. She must not like that people still remembered Etienne's former title. And here he'd thought that was the only reason she liked him – like a prized hound captured and used against its former owner. Or like one of these horses.

He clicked his tongue and the horse began to walk. He negotiated the way through fleeing people with care and came out on the other side to where the fields were broad and still dormant from winter but easy enough to ride over.

The delegation from Choan was riding over them toward him. And it was an impressive delegation, despite the fact that none of them could ride any better than he could. And yet, he suspected they did not mean to be impressive. They had the casual air of people fulfilling a troublesome task, not the feeling of a group puffed up with self-importance.

Their leader was surprisingly like Liandari, despite being male to her female, Two swords crossed in sheaths on his back and his dark blue coat hugged his figure snugly with slits cut for movement if he decided to start slicing off heads with those swords the way she was liable to do.

Etienne felt more grateful than ever for the sharp black jacket that Allegra had given him. It was hard to sit as straight as he would like with rippling stabs of pain running through him and sweat from the pain breaking out across his forehead, cooling, and then blossoming again, but at least the coat was fine and black – suiting a man of station with a serious nature.

There were five of them riding toward him. He didn't glance backward to see if Allegra had sent any guards with him. It would make him look weak. And it didn't matter anyway. If these men were here to cut him down, they could do it easily, guards or no. If they were not here for that, a few extra bodies would not impress them.

Odd that Allegra hadn't given him orders on how to represent her. Not that it mattered. Whether he pretended to dance to another's tune or not, he would still negotiate for his own ends. Even Marielle had known that about him. Likely, Allegra did, too. She seemed to understand him in a way that few people did – thought she hadn't forgiven him for his choices.

He was more a convict on parole than a trusted ally as she waited for him to prove he was her creature. He'd have to dance a fine line of pretense and manipulation to maintain this tenuous hold on a single string of power. But one string would be enough. With one string he could begin to weave until every web was his again.

He could feel himself already smiling as he drew his horse up in front of the five Retribution representatives. At least the horse understood reining.

"I am Etienne Velendark, former Lord Mythos of Jingen, Ambassador of the Lady Saga and at your disposal," he said as grandly as he could. Some people were impressed with credentials. Best give them what they longed for, even while he despised them for wanting it.

"I am Ki'squall Tandari Felk of ship Salt Winds of the Shard Islands of the Eight Sea," the one who looked like Liandari said. Orange tattooing scrolled under his eyes – in a script Etienne did not know – and ran across the bridge of his nose. Other tattoos in black and green crept up from his collar to his jawline. Maps, no doubt. Like those Liandari and Anglarok wore. "Why do your people invade the land across the river?"

"Invade? We flee." Etienne kept his tone cool. It was best to admit nothing until he knew what they wanted.

"We demand you return to your city. This countryside will be overrun too quickly, and Choan is not prepared to house so great a population."

"I'm afraid that our people cannot return to Xin until we return to rebuild it," Etienne said calmly. He would look like a fool indeed if he was wrong – but he wouldn't be wrong.

"Rebuild it? Are you mad?" the Ki'squall looked toward the towering city across the river, intact and gleaming in the noonday sun.

"I am afraid that we will have to find other habitable lands until that time," Etienne said gravely. "We urge you to allow the population of Choan to do the same, and to remove your fleet from the coast of that great city as quickly as possible."

"Is that a threat?" the Ki'squall hissed.

Etienne raised an eyebrow. "Do you consider warnings to be threats? I've always thought a friendly warning was a sign of friendship."

"A warning? Is your madness spreading then?" The curl of the Ki'squall's lip was jeering, but his eyes widened suddenly as the ground under them shook.

Etienne's gaze whipped to Xin, his heart freezing in his chest even as his horse danced fearfully under him. There was a creaking, scraping, mud-sucking sound and then people were scrambling up from boats onto the shore as fast as their legs could carry them while other boats rowed for this side of the river for all they were worth. A wave shoved them forward, but Etienne knew from grim experience that in only a moment it would suck them backward again.

They hadn't been fast enough in evacuating the city. He swallowed back a heart-rending pang. Those emotions were a waste of his time. If he were to rule well, he must do it with a cool head.

And then the head of the dragon rose, its eye opening. He shook his head violently, sending buildings, boats, bridges, and bits of wall flying from his face like droplets of water from a shaking dog.

Etienne barely kept on the back of his horse as it bucked and screamed. He bit his tongue as pain flared through his belly, tasting blood and spitting it to the side. The horse of the Ki'squall turned a wild eye on him as the man of the seas frowned, gripping the saddle with his free hand and turning pale with the effort of keeping his seat.

Debris rained down on them from the city above. One of the blocks of stone that had once graced a bridge or fine building fell from the sky, completely crushing one of the Retribution – horse and all. The stone was so large that not a sign of them could be seen once the dust cleared.

Screams filled the air as civilians fled, bringing crying children and panicked animals with them.

They should have been faster.

But there was no time for regrets.

"This is what we meant by rebuilding," Etienne said firmly over the stormy chaos.

The Ki'squall met his eye with a look of horrified surprise. "You knew? You knew this dragon slept under your city?"

"Not just under ours. One sleeps under Choan, too."

"And you knew it would rise?" He shouted back, sawing his horse's reins violently as he tried to bring the beast under control.

Etienne's own horse was still shaken. It skittered to the side as if it could dance its way completely off the surface of the earth.

He kept his grip on the reins firm. No need to overreact. That would only panic the horse more.

"We had barely the time to evacuate our people."

"People rain from the sky like a grisly squall," the Ki'Squall said through gritted teeth, his gaze turned to the sky.

Etienne refused to follow his gaze. Why break his own heart when he already knew what he would see?

Marielle had made this choice. She had killed in order to save. And he still wasn't sure if she'd made the right choice. What was so wrong with sacrificing five girls a year when it saved the lives of hundreds, hmm? He'd never thought the trade a poor one and he didn't think it was so bad even now.

And yet … how long can a society enslave itself knowing that eventually it must steel its nerve and win freedom through blood and agony? They simply had the misfortune of bearing the suffering now – in their generation.

"That is the warning I meant to give," Etienne said firmly. "Choan will rise soon. You and your people need to make arrangements. Flee the city. Take what you can."

"You just want to take the city back," the Ki'Squall said, his face flushed. "You know we mean to take every city on these plains for the honor of the People of Queen Mer."

"And this doesn't change your plans?" Etienne asked, pointing to the dragon above. It took all his nerve not to flinch as a brick fell one a span away from his horse, burying itself as deeply into the earth as it was thick. "This is the third dragon on the plains to rise. There are only two left. We are already ruined. There is nothing left here for you to take."

"Choan will not be affected by this grim fate," his enemy said, finally getting his horse under control and urging it up to join Etienne so they could speak without screaming. "Our leaders have taken care of everything needed to secure the city."

"It will not be enough."

"Again, you threaten us." His face bent into a snarl.

"Again, it is only a warning of a truth that is real. Before Springhatch, there won't be a city standing on these plains. All will have to be rebuilt. This is not what you came for. Why not go while you can?"

"You would destroy your own cities to keep us away?" he hissed.

Etienne's snort was mocking. "Just deliver the message." There was a thump as a body hit the ground beside them. Etienne had already seen a flash of petticoats. He refused to look. There was no point in paining himself more than he needed to. "Hopefully someone from Queen Mer's People is wiser than you are and will flee while he still can."

The Ki'squall spat on the ground. "We came to find the opener of the Bridge of Legends and we will not leave these lands until he is found."

Etienne felt a chill at those words. Now that Marielle had begun on this path, she needed to see it through. All this suffering had to be *for* something. Otherwise, he was nothing but an accomplice in the worst crime committed on these plains. And he could not allow that.

"What will you do with him when you find him?" he asked.

Perhaps, if Queen Mer's people were still here once all the dragons had been freed – perhaps it would be best to give them Tamerlan. He was far past saving now. And the plains would need to be free of madmen and villains to rebuild and find hope again. He would sacrifice anything for that. His own life – and the lives of all others.

"There is a prophecy. We are bound by it. And bound by secrecy," the Ki'Squall said.

Etienne turned his gaze upward. Nothing had fallen among them in a few moments. Perhaps the dragon was departing.

Yes. He swallowed down bile as he watched the mud-coated underbelly. The dragon swam through the sky to the northwest. He was already heading to the portal – he and all the helpless victims who had been unable to flee their city before it became their tomb.

"How convenient," he said dryly, wrenching his gaze from the horrific creature. It had never been intended for their world. But its removal was as painful as the removal of an organ.

The Ki'squall's gaze turned to the departing dragon and his throat bobbed as he swallowed down his own reaction.

His eyes turned bright and furious as he spoke, "He will open the Bridge, and in that day, it is only the Heir of Mer who may close it again. In retribution, the heir of Queen Mer will lay waste to the Legends and return the dragons to their place and they will be quelled forever, their fury kept at bay for all eternity. That's the prophecy, man of dust. Listen and be warned."

He turned, calling for those who still lived to follow him and rode toward Choan.

Etienne flexed his fingers, wishing – as he had a thousand times before – that he still had access to the magic of Jingen – or even just the power of a city at his back. He felt oddly vulnerable. And vulnerability was the one thing he could not afford.

15: From Depths to Heights

Marielle woke to pain in her lungs. She coughed violently, trying to rein it in. She failed. Coughs bent her double, tensing her whole body and clenching her eyes and fists shut. Between smoke inhaled, water inhaled, and someone trying to strangle her to death, her lungs had been through too much. Could they survive long enough to end this?

Strong arms held her as she coughed again, waiting until the agony of it subsided long enough to open her eyes.

"There you are, sweet Marielle," Tamerlan said, gently stroking her face. He looked rakish with the black patch over his eye. "You're with us. You're safe."

"Where are we?" she gasped.

"Still at sea. Jhinn is trying to navigate the rubble of Xin so he can bring us to Yan," Tamerlan said.

She struggled to sit, but he put a hand on her shoulder.

"Don't sit up, Marielle," his tone was dark. "There are things in the water you'd rather not see. Better to rest."

But she knew what he meant. When Jingen fell it had been him feverish in the bottom of the boat while she navigated between the bloated bodies of the dead and the floating rubble of what had once been their lives.

A pain – sudden and intense – seared her chest and her hand reached for the Windrose automatically. She hadn't felt a burst of pain from that since the Harbingers had tried to call her from on the dragon's back.

"My Windrose," she gasped, ripping her cloak and shirt aside to look at her chest. A flare of light greeted her. Tamerlan's face was bright in the glow of it, his concern painted across his face as plain as the sun in the sky.

"They're calling you again."

"But who? The only ones who knew I had this mark are dead!"

He shook his head, but the pain intensified. It was tugging her toward something.

"I need to go that way," she said, pointing north.

"To Xin?" Tamerlan's brow wrinkled. "The city is gone, Marielle."

"No," she gasped. Even talking hurt. "Further north."

She felt Tamerlan's kiss to her brow, but she saw Jhinn's drawn expression. He looked worried. His mouth opened and closed a few times as Tamerlan murmured to her, "Of course."

"Not 'of course'," Jhinn interrupted. "It's a bad idea, Marielle. We should go to Yan first. We can talk to your mother there. It's the easier avatar to find." He shot a wary glance at Tamerlan. "There's no point trying to hide what we're doing from Tamerlan anymore. He knows."

She tried to nod, but the pain was too much. Instead, she settled for gripping Tamerlan's hand in both of hers and squeezing as hard as she could.

"I think she's in a lot of pain." Tamerlan's voice was always calm and steady. So strange when she remembered that he was fighting a never-ending internal battle. "I have a feeling that she has no choice in the matter."

Sweat broke out across her forehead.

"We all have choices," Jhinn said, his voice rough. "What we did back there was a choice. People died. People suffer right now – a lot more than Marielle is suffering – as a result of what we did."

"Sure," Tamerlan said, placating him now. "But you have to go to Choan eventually, right? You have to deal with the Admiral."

"The Admiral is on our side. We should leave him until the end. He can help you as an ally inside your own mind."

Tamerlan tensed at that and Marielle longed to look in his eye, but her own eye was squeezed shut. She could hardly think, her breath coming in gasps as they sped *away* from the pull when all she needed with all her being was to speed *toward* it.

"You don't know what a Legend wants until it tries to spend your soul to have it. The Admiral might have fought for us in the past, but that doesn't make him our ally," Tamerlan said grimly.

"He's more your ally than Lila is. I hear the threats she breathes in your ear. Even now she is telling you how she will make you dance to her tune as soon as you have the Admiral and Ram destroyed. She says the crown is hidden where no one will ever find it and so she will always possess you."

"Sometimes I forget that you can hear them, too." Tamerlan's voice was both regretful and oddly grateful.

"Please," Marielle gasped. She hadn't meant to. She wasn't in control of herself anymore. She shook with tremors from deep in her core, heat washing over her making her muscles like liquid.

"Every Legend is a threat, Jhinn," Tamerlan said gently. Perhaps it would be best to go to Choan and deal with the Admiral first."

There was a long silence where Marielle could hear nothing but her boots bumping against the hull as she shook, Tamerlan's comforting shushing sounds and the whirr of Jhinn's pedal-powered motor. And then he finally spoke. He sounded almost painfully serious.

"Etienne thought we should kill you to destroy their access to this world. Marielle thought you could help instead. Tamerlan, you are my friend and closer than a brother. I do not see the Legends as the threat that Marielle and Etienne do and I never have. Which is why this whole … thing … with them has been I don't know, hazy. It's been hazy to me. These people of the plains are not my people. I've never really cared about them – they're the dead. Not a part of life. But it turns out that the dragons are a part of it. I care about them. I must see them free. And though you are like a brother to me, things changed when I learned the great truth."

"Meaning that you'll kill me yourself if you need to in order to open the water between worlds for your people," Tamerlan replied. Marielle's eyes shot open with his words.

"Yes."

"I accept that."

"Please," she begged again, but now she didn't know if she were begging for herself or Tamerlan or someone else.

"Kill me, if you must, Jhinn," Tamerlan said quietly. "But you can't go on the land. And Marielle is in too much pain to go on land for you unless we take her where she wants to go. So, either we take her north and you trust her to do the right thing or we keep going east and then you'll have to trust me."

Jhinn grunted. And then the boat turned in the water and Marielle felt a momentary lessening of the pain as they changed course.

"It's not that I don't trust you, Tamerlan," Jhinn said. "It's just that it's not always you that I'm dealing with. And I heard what Lila just said. I know that she will kill me if she can."

Tamerlan shuddered at Jhinn's words, but he drew Marielle in closer so that she could cling to him as she rode the waves of pain that rippled through her chest as the noose around it drew her ever northward.

"As long as I think with my own mind and feel with my own heart, I am yours, Marielle," he whispered. Devotion radiated off him in ripples of daisy scented pearl that laced itself around his golden scent and seemed to almost root itself within him so that all she could smell was his firm commitment as she clung to consciousness. "I will keep you as safe as I can and help you as much as I can until the Legends finally take me and Jhinn or Etienne or you must slay me."

She moaned, the pain too much to speak – not just physical pain anymore, but the emotional pain his words brought. There had to be some way to do this that didn't mean his death. There just had to be.

She drifted in and out of reality, feeling his kissed on her forehead in her conscious moments as he kept her close.

Memories of diving deep, deep, under the sea with Jhinn, surfaced. She remembered the gleam of treasures within the Pirate's cave. She remembered the way they'd fought the sea to shatter his avatar, the form of its hardened flesh crumbling like broken coral in their hands as they wrenched it from the cage.

But this time when she pulled it apart, the avatar wore Tamerlan's face.

This time, when she sucked in water and nearly drowned, she sucked in bits and pieces of what was left of him.

"It's okay, Marielle," she heard him croon to her. "You will do what you must, and I will help you. My dying breath will be yours."

She saw herself killing him in her mind's eye, her hands wrapped around his throat, her knife slicing into his skin, her sword piercing his heart. And each time she saw herself kill him, a new wound ripped across her soul.

There just had to be some other way.

16: Touch of Queen Mer

Strangely, Choan had changed very little considering it was occupied by invaders from across the ocean. It was clear at once that it was occupied, but the buildings and structures remained mostly intact. Ships still sailed in and out of the harbor. Guards were posted at the gates.

There was, however, an orderly but steady stream of small craft leaving the city packed to the rails with people.

Jhinn's gondola was stopped by a family boat with a blustering man at the helm.

"Ho there, Waverunner!" he called to Jhinn.

"I see you, brother."

"Change course, boy!" the man said with a friendly smile. "Haven't you heard the news from Jhinn of Jingen? We had a boat come to the city from Xin only yesterday. The Waverunner piloting it told us he'd heard word from this Jhinn that all the stories and prophecies have been made true. Our faith is complete. We set course upriver to the mountains to join the great waters of beyond!"

"Then I wish you well," Jhinn said and Tamerlan shared a smile with him. The word was spreading.

Fools! They join the dragons to their own doom. Ram's mutterings were almost constant now.

Cold instantly filled him. Unless all the dragons were freed, all these people would have their hopes and faith dashed on the rocks of the mountain city. And right now, the hopes of that were looking grimmer. Marielle had lost consciousness hours ago and he could barely keep the Legends at bay. They had kept him awake all night breathing threats in his ears and when he had nearly drifted off to sleep, Lila had tried to take his body – and nearly succeeded. It had taken all his efforts to beat her back and now he didn't dare drift off again, not even for a moment.

And how long do you think that will last? Everyone must sleep.

Her mental voice caressed him, as if she could lull him to sleep with her words.

I can wait, and I will. You are no Legend, only a boy. And a boy who will give in eventually. You think you are winning because you have destroyed avatars, but haven't you noticed that with every one you destroy, the ones who remain become stronger? We no longer need you to smoke to open the Bridge. We can take you and hold you against your will. And that was before Deathless Pirate was gone. Now, when you lose concentration for even a moment, even to sleep, we have the chance to grab

Her laughter sent jagged spikes of fear through every part of him, but he didn't dare surrender to it. Not now. Not ever.

He'd just have to stay awake. For as long as possible.

A pair of guards stopped them. They wore only voluminous trousers and carried harpoons, their stony gazes unmoving. Their bare chests were so covered in tattoos that he couldn't tell what color their skin was. Coastlines bled into strange birds and flowers and even monuments and curling waves.

"By order of Admiral Black Sails, no new travelers are to be allowed into the city. Full evacuation has been ordered," the nearest one said, his face – dark with the scrawl of tattoos – was unreadable.

"We have to get in," Tamerlan protested. "Can we speak to this Admiral Black Sails?"

"No."

"Can we speak to your commander?"

One of the guards chuckled. "Our Ki'squall does not speak to riff-raff. Be gone with you and be glad you've had warning. Did you spy the ruins of the other city as you passed? It lifted up into the air and flew. If this city does the same, you'll be entreating the Legends to favor me for what I've done for you today."

Marielle moaned and Tamerlan clutched her tighter to his chest. A magical glow shone from her coat – glowing brighter the closer they came to the city until they arrived at this gate.

"She was marked by your people," Tamerlan said softly, gently pulling back the collar of her coat to show the marks. He'd traced those marks with a finger only a few nights ago. They'd been nothing more than a beautiful decoration then. Now, they seared her skin in lines of glowing agony. "And the mark draws her here. Surely, you can let her in."

The guard leaned over the boat, studying the glowing tattoo before he grunted and turned to his fellow guard.

"I'll go report to the Ki'squall," the other guard said stiffly. Both of them looked at Marielle like you might look at a cat who started speaking in the human tongue. He trotted away down the lip of the canal almost before he was done speaking.

"What is her name?" the remaining guard asked.

"Marielle Valenspear. Do you know why her tattoo is causing her so much pain?"

"Deep calls to deep. The sea calls in her debt. This happens sometimes."

The sea was calling in her debt? That didn't sound good. They had enough trouble on their heels already. Concern ripped at him as he watched her but just as suddenly a stab of someone else's thoughts shot through him and his fingers turned leaden. It was all he could do to shove the specter back, his shoulders and head drooping at the effort.

Next time you will be mine, Ram said in his mind, firm and confident.

They were eroding him moment by moment, but he didn't dare give in.

He clutched Marielle to his breast, as the sweat formed on his brow. To my last breath, Marielle, I am yours. To the last flare of thought in my mind. To the last drop of blood in my veins.

You're a fool. You gamble the lives of thousands on one transitory love. How many died when Xin rose in the air? It didn't have to be that way. You could have let the dragon sleep. You could have let Deathless Pirate live on. You're both instruments of wickedness and the downfall of nations.

He didn't know when he started shaking or how long he crouched in the bow of the gondola waiting for the Ki'squall while he trembled and fought to keep sane.

It was growing dark when Jhinn crouched down beside him.

"Do you want something to drink?"

"Hmmm?" His heart was racing. Could you have a heart attack from fighting within?

"I have water." Jhinn's eyes squinted as they assessed him.

"Trying to see if you have to kill me yet?" Tamerlan asked dryly. "It's not time yet, my friend. But we should give some water to Marielle."

Jhinn grunted. "We should probably tie you up, but I think the guards would find that suspicious."

They'd been stashed to the side as they awaited the Ki'squall.

Jhinn brought the waterskin and Tamerlan gently let some water trickle down his finger and into Marielle's dry lips. She sucked at his finger as he dribbled a little more past her lush lips, but he was worried about her. How bad was the pain if it kept her unconscious? He smoothed her hair back and wiped her brow. She wasn't looking well. Why put this mark on her and waste her like this?

He looked up at the wall with fury pulsing through him.

"You sure you're still sane?" Jhinn whispered. "Because you look like you might lay siege to this city all on your own. I'm not sure if you've noticed but they are making us wait for good reason. Most of the citizenry has left the city walls. The voices and bodies lessen by the hour. And I've been watching the ships leave the harbor. This is good, Tamerlan. When this dragon rises, the deaths of innocents will be far fewer than they have been before now – if there are any at all. Aren't you happy not to have this on your conscience?"

That all made sense. He should be happy. But mostly he was worried about Marielle. She looked so ill. She was so pale. What if the guards didn't let them through in time? What if she died like this?

He swallowed, standing on wobbly legs. Maybe there was a way to get her into the city without the agreement of this Ki'squall.

He was just going to have to defy them and enter the city anyway. He couldn't hold off the Legends and fight for Marielle much longer. He could feel exhaustion pulling him toward sleep. He needed to act while he still could. He was running out of time.

He blinked as a man appeared before him. Had Tamerlan's mind been wandering so far he hadn't seen the approach? The man was dressed like Liandari had been in a long dark coat with rows of silver buttons and slashes at the hips and under the arms to make movement easier. Tattoos in a light orange traced a line under his eyes and across the bridge of his nose.

Tamerlan blinked, trying to gather his thoughts. He needed to plead his case to this man. He needed to be bold and charming. He tried to smile, but instead, his words came out as a plea.

"Please. Please, listen."

"I am Ki'squall Tandari Felk of ship Salt Winds of the Shard Islands of the Eight Sea," the man said. "Charged with overseeing the abandonment of this city and the gathering of the Last Defense."

"The 'Last Defense'?" Jhinn sounded so alert and sharp.

"We are gathering a small group of our people to defend the avatar of this city. Foreigners are not among them. You must turn your boat around."

"How are you calling them?" Jhinn asked. "With a glowing mark of pain?"

"What?" the man asked. But surely the guards must have mentioned it to him.

Tamerlan tugged down the collar of Marielle's shirt to show the bright glow of her map tattoos. She moaned, eyes fluttering open for a moment.

The Ki'squall said something in another language that sounded like a curse.

"Get her inside. Do you know the way to the palace?"

"Yes," Tamerlan said.

See? They gather their best and brightest to defend the avatar here. You will not destroy the Admiral. You will not destroy any of us before we take you once and for all.

"Then hurry. Clearly, fate has determined that she will stand with us. I've seen the tug of the Windrose, but I've never seen such an extreme case. You need to hurry. No, wait." He flung up a hand as Jhinn began to leave. "I'll come, too." He threw a dark-eyed look at the guards. "No one else re-enters the city. You have your orders."

He leapt into the boat, standing at the bow as Tamerlan settled back down to the floor of the boat and Jhinn leaned into the pedals.

"An interesting motor you have there, boy," he said as they pedaled into the lock and waited for the man in the little shed beside the lock to operate the wheel and raise the water level so they could enter the city. "Where did it come from?"

"I made it," Jhinn said shortly. Tension was in his every movement. And no wonder. He could barely look at the Ki'squall, he hated them so much. Heretics. Tamerlan had almost forgotten that Jhinn saw them that way. To him, they were worse than the dead men who walked the earth because they *could* have been alive and chose death instead.

"You could make a fortune selling them in Quavitlos or Xytexyx," the Ki'squall said.

Jhinn seemed to shrink from his words.

Tamerlan cleared his throat, trying to diffuse what could be a difficult situation. "You said you've never seen such a strong pull on a Windrose. Is something wrong? Will it kill her?"

The Ki'squall shook his head, but his brow was furrowed. "I don't think so. They aren't made for that. They are made to call the Windseeker or so that fate may draw them to the place they most need to be. But I've never heard of anyone dying from that. In fact, stories of such a strong reaction as this one are exceedingly rare."

"Rare," Tamerlan repeated as his heart sank. That didn't sound hopeful at all. If it was rare, then no one was going to know how to fix it.

"Usually it's just a pull. An undeniable pull. It's possible that if you fought against the pull you could harm yourself, but no one fights it."

"Because they know that they have to follow?"

"And because it's their duty to follow," the Ki'squall agreed. "Did she fight the pull?"

"There are things we have to do …" Tamerlan's voice trailed off. They should have noticed right away and done something.

They should have known that Marielle would have been fighting it on her own and that she wouldn't have let them see the fight until she was losing. That sounded much more like her.

See how all her fighting only made it worse? That was Lila in his mind. Your fighting is the same. Each battle only wounds you further. Surrender to us. Surrender and we will give you money and prestige. We may even keep the girl for you.

I want her as avatar. That was Ram growling.

Another can be found as an avatar. He could keep her on the side.

And who will make love to her? You? Ram sounded furious. We will never give him his own hands back to caress her with or his own lips to kiss her with. I'm not so cruel as to tease him with false hope. She is nothing but a complication. Best to use her as an avatar.

Perhaps the Admiral will be affectionate to her, Lila suggested. *If it pleases Tamerlan, it's a small thing to allow.*

We won't be letting him *have control, either. He's not of us. He's from another world and time.*

Tamerlan tried to force their voices away, but they only faded a little.

"You should have followed the first pull of the Windrose," the Ki'squall said as they sped down the canal. It was almost shocking to see how empty the city was. They saw only one boat headed the other way and packed with people – the homeless, tattered and barely holding the rails and the Retribution who had clearly found them in the alleys and under the bridges of Choan – a barge. The rest of the canals were empty.

Wind howled down the empty streets, sending an empty basket tumbling all the way down the length of it. It didn't catch on a street vendor cart because there wasn't a single one in the streets.

The silence was deafening.

In one window, a rug hung forlornly as if someone had hung it in the morning to air out and then fled without remembering to bring it back in the house – or possibly without caring to do so. Why tend to a rug you couldn't take with you when your whole city was forfeit?

Well, we could just let her live, Lila said after a long moment. Tamerlan tried to block her out as he gently caressed Marielle's hair, but it was impossible to block out your own thoughts. *I think Tamerlan would like that, hmm? That won't really inconvenience us. Just surrender, Tamerlan and I will let your girl live,* Lila said. *She can go and be a Scenter in whatever new City Watch they make. She'll be happy and you won't have to kill her. I'll even fake your death for her and she can go remarry some nice strapping young man with shoulders like yours and … well, it will be best for everyone.*

But Marielle wouldn't go of her own free will. She was more determined than a terrier with a rat in its teeth, clutching it to the death. And if Ram the Hunter took him and not Lila Cherrylocks, then he would destroy Marielle. He glanced back at Jhinn who was shaking his head wildly.

That's why you need to choose me, pretty boy, Lila said. *While you still have a choice between Ram and me.*

There is no choice …

Ram's mental voice kept ringing in his head long after he was done speaking … or maybe he was chanting the words because all Tamerlan heard as they proceeded through the empty city was: *there is no choice, there is no choice, there is no choice.*

He heard it as they swept through the rest of the city, speeding down canals usually packed with traffic. He heard it as they swept through the unguarded archway that led into the canals of the palace. He heard it as he lifted Marielle in his arms, cradling her as he stepped from the gondola to the platform beyond. He heard it as Jhinn made a displeased sound in the back of his throat.

"There's always a choice," Jhinn said aloud, his face dark with concern as he peered past Tamerlan to an open door where a ring of the Retribution stood around a cage made of bone. "Don't forget that."

Tamerlan tried to nod, but it was hard to think with the words still echoing in his mind.

17: THE HEART OF CHOAN

MARIELLE

Pain rippled through her mind, pounding, pounding in her skull until her very teeth ached with it. Thoughts had fled hours ago. Or maybe it was minutes. She felt like she'd been in pain a lifetime or an hour or … time was meaningless in the depths of pain. It no longer ticked to a familiar rhythm, no longer slipped away with idle thoughts and daydreams. It marked the seconds like they were hours. It drew out minutes like years. It was everything and nothing. It ate her away until she was only pain frizzling and agonizing at every edge and point.

And then there was less pain. She could almost breathe as it lifted. She could almost think.

She felt arms around her – stable and secure, warm and affectionate. They cradled her against a muscular chest and she sighed into its strength and warmth. Tamerlan. When she surfaced it was always Tamerlan who was there. Who wouldn't want to keep that forever?

And she could. He was her husband, her deepest love and that meant she could keep him forever.

She let herself breathe, exhaling the pain, inhaling new hope. Her skin across her neck and chest was still tender, but her mind was clearing. Little shivers of hope rocketed through her like comets. She couldn't quite catch them, but they were there again.

She could feel movement now – the gentle rolling of steps as she was carried. Voices rose around her.

"This way, foreigner. Bring her here. We make preparations for the unthinkable."

"And what is that?" Tamerlan asked, his deep voice rumbling through his chest against her ear. Her breath hitched a little at the joy of hearing it again. She'd been worried back there on the island – worried that he would be lost to the Legends so quickly. But he was still here. Still himself. Still sane.

She let her eyes flutter open to see a man dressed like Liandari leading them through an open door into the massive Grand Hall of the palace. She smelled Jhinn behind her, his scent a tangle of concern and anxiety. It was hard to even see the details of the hall with the strong scent of anticipation masking everything else and clouding the room in the spring green color of its scent. Tamerlan's scent – as intoxicating as ever and mixed now with threads of devotion and loyalty every time he looked at her – spiked with the insanity scent she'd started to associate with Legend, but it was nothing compared to what was in the Hall – there was something with a scent so strong that it was cutting through that spring green color. She squirmed to get a better look at where that scent was coming from.

"Easy, Marielle," Tamerlan's whisper gusted across her cheek sending little goosebumps over her flesh. "It's okay, sweet love of my life. I've brought you where you need to be."

But she was distracted from the shivers his words stirred in her by the ring of men and women surrounding a bone cage. Suspended, inside was a glowing aqua specter – a man dressed like the Ki'squall but more elaborately. He knelt in the cage, frozen with his head tilted all the way back and a scream in his throat.

She'd seen this being created through Tamerlan's eyes when they made their Admiral into an avatar. She choked back rising terror at the sight of it, her insides trembling uncomfortably at the sight and her stomach heaving.

"Set me down," she gasped through a raw throat. "I can walk."

Tamerlan set her down instantly – steadying her with his hands as she wobbled on weakened legs. Nausea roared through her, making her head light, but she fought against her bucking stomach. Tamerlan leaned in close, as if he could shelter her with his body, his eyes earnest as they locked on hers.

"Are you … can you stand?"

"Yes," she breathed, grateful that he was blocking the view of the avatar.

"I was worried about you," he whispered. "You are my life, Marielle."

He took her face in a hand, caressing her cheek with his thumb as his fingers threaded through her hair to cup her ear. Not caring at all about the audience watching him, he leaned in, pulling her to his chest and bent to kiss her – softly, tenderly at first but with growing urgency.

And then he shook, as if with some diseased tremor.

She pulled back with a gasp. His eye shuttered painfully, and he hissed in the back of his throat, snatching his hands from her as if she were burning hot. The agony on his face was painful to watch.

"Tamerlan?" she asked, hearing her voice quaver.

His good eye spun wildly, the other covered by its black patch.

"Run!" he gasped.

She was frozen in place. What should she do? Did he see some danger behind her? She spun, but there was nothing behind her except for that hideous avatar and the ring of the Retribution standing to guard it. They drew their weapons, the sound of steel whispering into the descending night. They were all standing on the defensive, though, not like they were going to attack her.

She was already shaking her head in confusion when she turned back to Tamerlan, but the gaze she met was not his. It was steely hard, a glimmer of rage in the depths of his eyes. He slid his own blade free, a cruel sneer on his face.

She stumbled backward, panic thickening her tongue and making her legs heavy and clumsy.

No.

Not this.

They had him. Somehow, they'd taken him against his will.

But who was it?

"Lila," she asked tentatively.

His laughter was harsh and mocking. "You wish."

She was still fumbling for the knife in her belt as one of the Retribution called out, "Treachery!"

They surged past her.

"He used the girl with the Windrose to get past the guards. Someone, grab his gondola!"

There was a scream as she raised her dagger – just in time to see Tamerlan carve his sword through one of the Retribution with the smooth efficiency of a butcher. She gagged as the man fell, eyes lifeless and body mangled.

If that wasn't Lila, then it certainly wasn't the Legend raised from among these people. And that meant it was Ram. Ram, who wanted more than any of them to stop her and imprison the dragons forever.

Her breath hitched in her throat and she spun, turning her back on them all and rushing over to the bone cage. This wouldn't be as simple as destroying Deathless Pirate had been. The cage was locked, and her arms couldn't reach through the bars.

There was a trick to this. She remembered watching Carnelian pick locks. She could do it. She just had to focus.

Behind her, Tamerlan grunted and someone screamed. Ram was winning. He always won. She jiggled her knife into the lock trying to ape what she'd seen the guardswoman do. Just like this … and then this…

The knife popped out, slicing her thumb wickedly and she gasped.

The door of the cage swung open with a snick of the lock.

Blood. It was always blood when it came to magic. She scowled as she opened the door. Could no one think of a peaceful solution? Must it always be blood and gore and death? She bit her lip, hearing herself as she eased into the cage beside the shade of what had once been a man. Here she was, disdaining violence and she was about to destroy the remnant of this man. Ridiculous. Weak.

She shook her head at herself. Glancing nervously over her shoulder to see Tamerlan holding off two of the Retribution, his blade so fast she couldn't keep track of it. His gaze met hers – violent and full of rage. She shuddered and spun back to the avatar.

"Don't!" he roared from across the room. "Don't you dare touch him!"

She fumbled with the door of the cage, shutting it behind her with an ominous click. That should buy her more time. Somehow. But how would she destroy this Legend? Deathless Pirate had been simple. One blow to his disintegrated body and it had shattered into a thousand lifeless shreds. This one was half-there still. Like a corpse that had not yet putrefied.

Swallowing, she tried stabbing it with her dagger. The dagger caught in the chest of the avatar – substantial enough to provide some resistance, but not enough to harm him. She drew it out and slashed his throat, biting her lip with horror as she did it. It tore like slashed meat – and that was all. Nothing. No blood. No death. Nothing.

Sobbing tearlessly, she grabbed the avatar and tried to shake it, but it felt dead in her hands, lifeless, useless. This was not what she expected at all.

The screams behind her had quieted. She had only moments.

Desperately, she sawed at the neck of the avatar, her knife too small for the task of decapitating what had once been a human being. Her cuts were rough and raw-edged.

She heard the cage behind her snick when she still wasn't through the spine. She dropped the knife and grabbed the head in both hands, wrenching it from the body and letting out a warbling cry of horror as it finally came loose. The light around the avatar faded at the same time that the body tumbled forward, a sea of black pearls pouring from the open neck and flooding the bottom of the cage, spilling out onto the floor beyond.

What in all the starry skies was this?

She flung the head away like it could infect her with evil. It landed in the sea of pearls, mouth opening and more pearls spilling onto the floor of the cage. She stumbled to the side, wiping her hands on her trousers and vomiting into the pearls.

She had just done the unspeakable. She had just damned herself in every possible way.

She would have collapsed, but the cage door squeaked open and violent hands grabbed her by the shoulders and dragged her from the cage, flinging her out the door and onto the ground. She skidded through blood and gore, and rolling black pearls, trying not to see what was all around her, what she was practically bathed in.

The hall was silent except for her panicked breathing and the sound of the cage being slammed shut.

"It took them hours and all the magic they had to make that avatar," Ram said with Tamerlan's voice. He leaned over her, his eyes inches from hers as he spoke and she shuddered, a cry of terror ripping through her as she shut her eyes against that look on his face. The face that should have meant warmth and comfort. The face that meant the end of her. "I will work much more quickly."

He pulled her up from the ground violently, shoving her in front of him. She fought against his grip, her hands – slick with blood – fighting for purchase and finding nothing.

It was no use.

Tamerlan was already much stronger than she was, but possessed by Ram he was Legendary. He slammed her against the bone cage, and she saw stars as the back of her skull hit the bone with force. She blinked them back, retching as she tried to catch a breath that wasn't full of the smell of death.

Something caught her wrist, dragging it up to head-level and pinning it in place. She felt a sudden pressure and then she was caught – her hand tied to the cage with a blood-soaked leather belt. She barely had time to cry out before her other hand was imprisoned against the cage.

"These things take time – but the crueler the victim is treated, the quicker it happens," Ram the Hunter said with Tamerlan's lips. "We found that out the hard way. Fortunately, we know how to do this fast when we have to. And since you just woke this dragon – we have to do it right now. Let's see what depths of cruelty we can descend to, hmm? At least you'll have one thing to hope in – we'll have to do it fast."

She felt her eyes trying to roll back into her head. Felt her brain trying desperately to be anywhere but here. But there was nowhere else to be.

Tamerlan grabbed her leather vest and sliced the straps of the buckles holding it closed one by one, wrenching it open and exposing the pale skin beneath.

"Fast requires a lot of blood, too." He said it so factually, like he was reciting the Laws of Jingen and not describing the gruesome way he was about to murder her.

Her breath was spiraling out of control coming far too fast. She knew that, but she couldn't slow it down. The end was coming.

Tamerlan's face swam into view again and he had a curved dagger in his hand – possibly taken from one of the fallen Retribution.

"It's a pity it had to go this way. I wanted to use you to bind one of the already free dragons and now I have to waste you to bind this one." He shook his head like a patient teacher working with a misbehaving child.

And then his face took on a strange expression and he slumped to the ground.

18: SON OF MER

JHINN

The Retribution guard stood there, tense, one hand on the gondola, shock etched into his face as the last of his fellows fell to the ground. They could see it all happening through the doorway into the hall like a tiny but grisly street performance.

Jhinn gripped an oar in his hands, the blood draining from his face as one guard after another fell.

"You have to go help them!" he told the guard beside his boat.

"I was ordered here."

Of course. He gritted his teeth in frustration.

Why did he put any trust in the Retribution? Heretics were all the same – too cowardly to stick to principle. Too weak to hold to anything. They'd snap and like a broken sail rope and leave everything flapping in the wind the one time you relied on them. He clenched his teeth and watched as Tamerlan reached into the cage.

Beneath his boat, he felt the earth begin to tremble – or rather, the dragon Choan.

Sweat was forming along his brow and spine, despite the fact that he felt cold in the winter air.

"You must," he snapped at the guard. "You're here to defend this place, aren't you? Well, go defend it!"

"The avatar is already slain, fanatic," the guard said, disdain in his eyes as he watched Jhinn. He stepped into the gondola with authority. "You will take me out of this city on your boat or I will take this boat from you."

He would be no help at all.

Jhinn felt his mind turning like the oiled gears he'd used to make the motor. He could feel his options clicking into place. If he let this guard do as he wanted, they would abandon Marielle to her fate and with her, the fate of the dragons and his people. But he had no way to compel the guard. No way to save her or stop Tamerlan except to go in there himself. And no way to get there without dying – without standing on the land. With the Maid Chaos's people, they had carried him. His feet had never touched land. But this was different. He'd have to step willingly onto the ground.

He swallowed.

His people needed Marielle. She, alone, could speak to the dragons and ask them to bear his people up the waterfall. That had been his plan all along. To ask the dragons to help them rise up the mountain to escape with the dragons through the portal to the worlds beyond. If they couldn't convince them, then they couldn't ascend high enough to get to the portal at all. They would either be stranded here or break their vows and faithfulness.

And the only way to keep them all from heresy was if he stepped into it himself.

He wiped a hand across his brow. It had barely been a second since the guard spoke and yet it felt like hours as he weighed his choices. What would it mean if he chose to break his faithfulness for the sake of his people? Wouldn't that make him just as bad as the heretic in his boat right now?

No, because at least he was not a coward.

He clenched his jaw harder, but inside, his heart was breaking. He already knew what he needed to do.

And he hated himself already for the choice he was going to make. He hated himself because it felt like this act somehow undid all the other times he'd been faithful at great cost. Like he was denying everything he'd ever believed or hoped for in the acknowledgment that what was going on in that hall was real – wasn't just an illusion in the land of the dead – and that he could and should affect it with his choices.

He didn't realize he was crying until his eyes grew glassy and his grip shifted on the oar.

"We're going to fulfill my orders," the guard said, gesturing toward where his commander lay dead on the ground of the hall. He paused for a moment, as if with regret, and Jhinn swung.

His oar cracked the man in the back of the skull, sending him sprawling across the bow of the gondola. Like a shot, Jhinn leapt from the gondola, tears streaming down his face as he ran. His lungs screamed in protest – and no wonder! – as he sped through the land of the dead, abandoning himself and everything he'd ever been in one moment of insane dedication.

There were weapons scattered across the floor, but he clung to the oar as his bare feet slipped through the blood and skidded across the flagstones. Tamerlan didn't even turn as Jhinn raised the oar and smacked him in the back of the skull.

Had he killed his friend? He didn't dare check.

He rushed to Marielle, keeping his expression blank and his focus certain as he struggled to release the belts holding her in place.

"Jhinn!" her voice was half speech and half sob. "What have you done? You're on the land!"

"Come on," he said, stumbling over his own words as he tried to explain. "I need you to ask this dragon to bear my people up the waterfall. They have no way to go up it on their own."

"Tamerlan," Marelle reached for him, beginning to bend, but Jhinn grabbed her by the waist and pulled her away roughly.

"It's still Ram in there. He still wants you dead," he barked, dragging her across the flagstone. "Are you listening? I need you to talk to the dragon. Now. While he's close. While you can."

Of course she was upset. But if she didn't listen then his heresy was for nothing. He was already trembling at the possibility.

"You don't *know* that he's still possessed by Ram!" Marielle protested. "We can't leave him here!"

"He was about to eviscerate you," Jhinn said patiently, pulling her roughly through the carnage as he dragged her to the gondola. She was taller than him, and more muscled, but his will was stronger right now. "Listen to yourself! We must slay the last avatars. And we can't do that with him along with us. He understands. He told me so."

"I – " Her voice broke. They were leaving bloody footprints on clean flagstones by the time she recovered her voice. "We can tie him up. We can keep him bound. Surely that's better."

Beneath them, the ground began to shift.

"No time," Jhinn gasped, pulling her harder. "Please Marielle, please listen."

"I can't abandon him!" her cry was nearly a wail.

He stopped, turning her so he could shake her by the shoulders. "Look at me! I'm standing on ground! I am one of the dead! I have abandoned everything."

She sucked back a sob, making a hiccupping noise as it stuck in her throat, her gaze trailing down and then back up and then gasping as if she was just now coming to her senses.

His own cheeks were hot with the tears that streamed down them. Hot with the betrayals he was committing.

"Why – ?"

He made his words slow. Clearly, emotions had clouded her mind. "I need you to talk to the dragon. I know you can. Ask Choan to ferry my people up the waterfall."

She gasped.

"Please," he added.

Her gaze strayed to Tamerlan and her face was agonized as the ground bucked under them again.

Jhinn growled in the back of his throat, grabbed her around the waist and propelled her toward the gondola.

He lifted her and threw her into it as soon as they were close enough. The ripple through the flagstones buckled his knees but he recovered enough to jump after her, checking the pulse of the guard of the before he scrambled to his seat at the pedals and untied the boat. The man was still alive. Jhinn grimaced at the thought of saving an enemy over the friend who was unconscious back in that Hall. But did he have any right to hate this heretic so much when he was now a heretic, too?

The thought was like a knife to his heart.

He began pedaling as soon as his feet could find the pedals, frantically exiting the palace. He had a long way to go to get out of there and experience had taught him that dragons rose quickly when they awoke.

Marielle was silent, staring with empty eyes at the doorway to the hall in the palace. Even after they'd left the palace, she still stared in that direction as if by her focus and grief she could bring back the dead and make her husband sane again, as if she could erase the past.

She should know that was impossible. She should forget what happened in the lands of the dead as Jhinn did and cling only to life on the water.

He flinched at the thought.

Could he think that way anymore? Now that he was a heretic? Now that he had betrayed everything?

He could still feel the awful hardness of the stone beneath his feet – the deadness of it, the stillness of it. It had no life – not like the water. And he'd abandoned faithfulness to the water for something that was slipping through his fingers.

"Please," he begged aloud.

"He says he'll do it," Marielle said from where she sat, her hollow eye still staring at the spot from which they'd fled. Her voice just as hollow as that eye. "He'll bear your people up the waterfall."

Jhinn gasped. Hope filled him for a moment – golden and fresh as a sunrise.

She turned her dead eye on him. "I didn't know I could talk to the dragons down here. How did you know?"

He shrugged. "I just thought it would make sense that you could, since you could talk to the dragons up on the mountains."

"And you didn't think you should share this theory with me?" Her voice sounded dead.

"I did share it with you," he said, pedaling as fast as he could. Why were they fighting about this now? When they had to flee the city? Was this about Tamerlan?

"But not before hundreds of innocent people died as Xin lifted into the air. Didn't you think that maybe we could have asked him to take his time and kill fewer people?" Her tone was deadly cold.

He froze. He hadn't thought of that. As far as he knew, his people had all left that city. He'd worked hard to get them out. He hadn't given any thought at all to those in the dead lands.

"You let them die for nothing," she said, her voice hollow.

"I walked on the ground to save you," Jhinn reminded her.

"You walked on the ground to save your people, not me." Her voice was harsh. "And what about Tamerlan?"

"He was going to kill you. He killed all those guards."

She looked away, conceding his point. So why didn't it make him feel any better? He had a bitter taste in his mouth and when he tried to clench his jaw against it, he bit his own cheek and tasted blood. Blood like the salt in the water, salt and water and life and blood. His mind was skipping along thought like a flat stone flung across the canal.

He was dead now. Dead and alive again. Or maybe just dead. He didn't know which and the uncertainty was much worse than any accusations Marielle might fling at him.

But there were two avatars left to slay. And he would slay them, even if the act finished the job of damning him forever.

19: Regrets and Guilt

She had thought that the pain of the Windrose was as bad a pain as a human could suffer — that the pull of it in her chest was the strongest tug imaginable. She had been wrong. The agony that filled her now dwarfed that. She'd take that former pain gladly in place of this. The tug of the Windrose had been like a fishing line compared to the ship's cable that tore at her heart with every inch they moved from the palace. He was in there. Unconscious. Vulnerable. He would die taken completely by the Legends, helpless, suffering and there was nothing she could do to save him or to stop it.

She wished she could argue with Jhinn to turn him around, wished she could believe that would be the right thing to do. But she knew it wouldn't be.

May I rise now, human? Choan asked her.

No, he must not rise yet.

Bitterness laced her thoughts. Why hadn't she thought to ask Xin to wait? Why hadn't Jhinn told her that she could? She would hate him for all eternity for letting her take innocent lives when she could have saved them. Hate him forever for callously abandoning her beloved Tamerlan when he needed them the most.

She shot a burning gaze at Jhinn but he ignored her, pedaling as hard as he could. She hadn't told him that she asked Choan to wait for them to leave. Why make his life easier after he had destroyed hers?

A tiny part of her mind was reminding her that he'd also saved her life. Ram was about to execute her in the most horrific way possible. And he'd broken vows and creeds to stop that.

But even that was not enough to quell her heartbreak.

She moved to the man unconscious in the hull, turning him to a more comfortable position and gently dabbing away the blood on the back of his head. She'd almost forgotten about her own injuries, but when she was done binding his head, she bound the wounds on her hand. They would all heal. It was the wounds inside that would not.

Oddly, the Windrose had stopped burning, as if even that had given up on her.

She took off her ruined leather vest and dropped it into the water and then tried to clean her fur cloak and hair.

"You can get pretty later. After we've fled the city," Jhinn growled.

"You sound like Etienne," Marielle said frostily. "I'm just trying to wash the gore off my body is that so awful?"

He made a growling sound and she thought he might snap back but the man in the boat awoke with a startled cry.

"Where are you taking me?" He sounded dazed.

"Out of the city," Jhinn said. "Or were you looking forward to riding the dragon into the night?"

"Maybe *you* should," Marielle said. "He'll take you straight to your home between the worlds."

Jhinn spat.

"Or doesn't that matter to you anymore?"

Jhinn's face went pale. "I may not be welcome. I am one of the dead now."

"You're back on the water," Marielle said. "Doesn't that make you reborn?"

"It doesn't work like that. They sank my mother in the river for nonsense like that. Do you know what it's like to grow up the son of a heretic?"

"My mother was a prostitute," Marielle said frostily. She wanted to fight someone. She wanted to fight anyone. "I suppose it was much the same."

"I doubt it. Prostitution is legal in Jingen – or was before it was destroyed. Heresy is not legal among the Waverunners."

"You stepped onto the land," the guard said, startling them both. "You're a child of Queen Mer and yet you walked on the land."

"Yes," Jhinn snapped. His patience was a thin thing and Marielle felt her lips compressing as she watched him fray before her eyes. "What of it?"

"He will open the Bridge and in that day, it is only the Heir of Queen Mer who may close it again. In retribution, the heir of Queen Mer will lay waste to the Legends and return the dragons to their place and they will be quelled forever, their fury kept at bay for all eternity."

"What's that nonsense?" Jhinn asked. His face grew darker as the locks came into sight. They were almost out of the city.

I am rising now. You are almost to the river.

She felt the water tremble as the Harbinger said in awe, "The last prophecy of Queen Mer. You are fulfilling it in our time!"

"Hang on to the sides!" Marielle called. There was no time to dig into prophecies. The dragon was about to rise.

She'd been through this before. But it never got easier. The current grew stronger as the water level swelled and the dragon's head rose above the city.

Beside her, the guard began to scream and then they were airborne, shooting over the lock and landing awkwardly in the pool below, only to shoot the next lock, too.

"Almost there," Jhinn said, as if to himself. "Almost there."

They were in the bay with the ships deemed too unseaworthy to sail when the wings began to lift, and the dragon took to the sky. The sucking hole left behind dragged them backward into the muddy swirl of water and for long minutes it was all they could do to fight the current with motor and oars.

Eventually, the boat slowed, and Marielle looked up into the sky at the silhouette of the dragon as it swam across the sun.

I will fulfill my promise.

At least this time the city had been evacuated – by everyone but Tamerlan.

She felt her lower lip tremble and tears blinded her so that she couldn't see where they were going until Jhinn landed them on the bank of the river.

"Here is where you get out, heretic."

"I'm no more a heretic than you, Son of Mer," the guard said.

"Don't call me that," Jhinn snarled.

There was a murmur from the bank and Marielle looked up to see that Jhinn had landed them beside an encampment of refugees from Choan and with them was a contingent of the Retribution.

"What did you call him?" a man dressed like a Ki'squall asked.

"He's the Son of Mer! The man from the prophecy!" the guard said eagerly as he clambered out of the boat.

"Shove off before they keep us here," Jhinn ordered Marielle.

Even if she'd wanted to push off, she couldn't. Strong hands gripped the gunwales of the gondola.

"The Son of Mer? The one of prophecy?" a voice asked.

"Can he really be the one?" a woman asked, pushing past the guard. Her clothing was finer than the Ki'squalls, her hair clubbed back under a wide-brimmed stiff hat. "Speak man, are you the one spoken of in the prophecies?"

"I'm only a fool who doomed himself to be a heretic just like you," Jhinn snarled.

"He walked on land, even though you know they don't do that! Just like the prophecy says!" their guard said, quoting. "He will open the Bridge and in that day, it is only the Heir of Mer who may close it again. In retribution, the heir of Queen Mer will lay waste to the Legends and return the dragons to their place and they will be quelled forever, their fury kept at bay for all eternity. In that day the landless will walk on Land and will be called the Son of Mer. In his unfaithfulness, he will be faithful. In his damnation, he will bring salvation to all."

"What was that?" Jhinn asked, his face pale. He reached out of the boat and grabbed the guard's arm, drawing him close. "What was that you said?"

The man squeaked. "It's only the prophecy! Everyone knows it!"

"I've never heard those words spoken before," Jhinn said, but his gaze had turned inward, his brow furrowing. The guard squirmed his arm out of Jhinn's grip.

"But you are a Waverunner, yes?" the woman asked, a considering look on her face.

"Who are you, if you please?" Marielle asked her. Jhinn ignored them both.

"I am Captain Hi'lan'yilth of the Black Sails Division of Ships," she said and around her, the Retribution snapped to a form of attention, fists to heart before relaxing at her gesture of two waving fingers.

"He *is* a Waverunner, Captain," Marielle said.

"Then it's true." The Captain's face was harsh and weathered by sun and wind, but her eyes widened with almost child-like wonder. The Son of Mer has come. He will save us from the dragons!"

"It's what we're trying to do," Marielle said tiredly.

The Captain cocked her head to the side. "And you wear our Windrose. You are pledged to all that is truth and justice." She nodded, seeming pleased. "You are helping him in this goal?"

"Yes," Marielle agreed.

"Good. The Retribution is at your disposal. What do you wish of us?"

Around her, gasps filled the air at the Captain's declaration.

"One of these dragons is in your land across the sea," Marielle said. "Buried under your city."

"Xyteryx," the Captain agreed.

"Really?" one of the sailors behind her said. Hurried whispering and worried looks filled the crowd of Retribution along the shore. Perhaps this part wasn't common knowledge to their people.

"When we have finished," Marielle said, weighing her words carefully. "When we have finished removing the dragons from this land, we must see to that one, as well. We need some way to get to it. Some way to explain to the people there who we are and what we are doing."

The Captain nodded briskly.

"A moment." She waved to a guard and when he trotted up, she gestured to him. "Bring the purser and parchment."

"We need to go, Marielle," Jhinn said through gritted teeth. Even after everything that had happened, he viewed these people as enemies.

"Wait only a moment, Jhinn," she said, her steely gaze turning to him. Their quarrel wasn't over. "We'll need this help. Surely we can wait a few minutes for it."

"If they want to help, they should give us food and water," he snapped.

Marielle and the Captain shared a look. Marielle embarrassed and the Captain amused. She nodded to one of her people and he trotted off, reappearing only minutes later with a waterskin and a basket of food. He offered them to Marielle.

"Thank you," she said.

Jhinn's eyes were fixed on the horizon as a burly man with a wooden writing desk slung from a strap around his neck came hurrying up. He made a quick salute to the Captain and then pulled out a pen and parchment. She leaned forward, her pen scratching as she wrote on the parchment and then handed Marielle the letter.

"Give this to anyone with a rank of Captain or above and they will know what to do."

"Thank you," Marielle said again, and the Captain gestured to her guards.

"We will send guardians with you."

"No," Jhinn's tone was harsh.

"That would be wonderful," Marielle said.

"No!" This time he pushed off from the bank, already pedaling with all his might. Marielle's mouth fell open and she hastily made a salute to the Captain like the ones the guards had made.

"My apologies," she shouted as they sped away. "Thank you for your great generosity."

They were nearly out of earshot before she turned on Jhinn.

"Do you really think you're so much better than them? You walked on land, too!"

"To my deep shame."

"And you saw it was prophesied! All this was! The prophecy said that you save everyone with what you did! Isn't that right? Isn't it good? Isn't it worth it?"

He was silent.

"And don't you realize," she said with a cutting edge to her voice, "that now that Tamerlan is gone, we might not be able to free the last dragon? What if one of the Legends takes *him* over as a new avatar and we have no idea where he is or how to find him?"

At that Jhinn's gaze shot up, and she gasped as she realized his eyes were glassy with tears.

"Please," he begged. "Please just let this all be over."

She sagged, deflated. What did you say to that? After all, she felt exactly the same way. Just when this couldn't get any worse, it did. She couldn't fight with him. Not when he was just as broken as she was.

"I'll take a turn pedaling," she said eventually. "You should sleep."

She couldn't think of anything else to say as she took his place and began the endless crawl back up the river, toward the last standing city of the Dragonblood Plains.

20: The Welcome of Yan

MARIELLE

After days of pedaling up the river with Jhinn's dark looks and angry silences, the city of Yan should have been a welcome sight. For Marielle, the sight was bittersweet.

Children played along the shores of the river and despite the chill of too-early Spring, men fished from the banks with long rods and baskets. Even the refugee camps of tents and shanties that they passed as they moved closer to the city looked cheerful – their cookfires bright and their people bustling.

At least they wouldn't be made refugees twice – not really. These camps were far enough outside the city that they should survive the rise of the dragon here. Assuming she could find the crown. Which was a pretty big assumption since she wasn't nobility and didn't know where to start looking. She'd counted on having Tamerlan with her. A landhold's son would know where to start the search.

She hadn't realized how much she relied on him until now –
when he was no longer with them, maybe no longer alive. It
had been all she could do these past few days to keep her focus
as her thoughts turned often to the last time she'd seen him,
crumpled on the floor in a pool of blood.

Jhinn was no help. He was wrestling with his own demons,
refusing to say more than yes or no to her at any time. She
wished she could help him, but everything she touched fell
apart. The best she could do for him was to leave him alone.

She put her hand over her Windrose often and thought about
the Retribution and their prophecies, about swearing the first
time and receiving the rose and about her vows to Jingen and
the law of the city. They were all about justice. And that was
what she was clinging to, now. With nothing else left, she'd
been stripped down to that one last shred – her absolute
dedication to justice in the world. She could still get it for
everyone. She just needed to focus on the goal and not the
sacrifices.

She clung to hope like a barnacle to a ship and prayed that
justice was real and achievable. She'd mourn her dead later.
She'd mourn her scars later. For now, there was only justice,
singing to her like a siren in the sea.

The city walls rose up – imposing but elegant – as they passed
the last shanty village and into the city. Beautiful though it was,
the presence of so many people made her lift her veil – growing
tattered now from so many months of use – to guard her nose.
Cities were always overwhelming and after days on the river,
she knew that so many emotions might overwhelm her.

Stern guards lined the gate, watching the passing boats. There were far more than she would have expected – rough men in untidy uniforms and Yan City Watch Officers with grim expressions backing them up. A long polearm blocked their passage.

"No new refugees. The city is full," the guard said, frowning at their gondola. "You'll have to apply for a day pass to trade in the walls."

"We're not refugees," Marielle said. "We're visitors."

He snorted. "A likely story."

Marielle felt her cheeks grow hot. She'd done her best to patch and clean the clothing she'd taken from Allegra's shops, but it hadn't been possible to entirely repair the effects of the battle while they were on the river. She didn't look like a former watch officer anymore, never mind a prosperous merchant or landhold.

"Name who you are visiting."

Her mind raced. She could give her mother's name, but what chance was there that a gate guard would believe that. As she bit her lip, her veil slipped and the scents of the city hit her like a gust of wind.

"Marielle?" a voice asked from among the guard and a woman stepped forward, lowering her own veil as she took Marielle in.

"Alyssan!" Marielle's eyes widened. She barely knew the other woman beyond her name, but she'd been a Scenter in the City Watch of Jingen.

"She's from the Jingen Watch," Alyssan said to the other guards. She turned to Marielle. "There are positions open here if that's what you're looking for, but you'll have to get cleaned up first. You're a wreck."

Marielle nodded seriously. "Thank you."

"Once you're tidy, report to Captain Longweather in the Alchemist's District. She's hiring more Scenters for the Springhatch Festival. I'm sure she'll offer you the role."

"Thank you," Marielle said, truly touched. In any other circumstances, she would have leapt at this. Imagine serving in the City Guard again – enforcing the laws and ensuring justice, polishing leather and armor before going out on patrol, drinking and eating with friends after a long day. She almost sighed at the thought, but Jhinn was pulling away from the cluster of guards and heading into the city.

"I guess you still have friends," he remarked, bitterly.

Marielle had almost forgotten about the Festival, but it was upon them already. Eggs, hollowed and painted, were strung on yellow ribbons over windows and doors. Clusters of dried herbs were tied along longer ribbons that were strung from rooftop to rooftop. It was a plea to the ages for newness and Spring. For rebirth and fresh starts.

Little arrows were painted on the eggs – a tribute to Byron Bronzebow who supposedly began the Festival when he brought stolen eggs by the cartload to a starving village. He'd plundered the eggs from a supply train headed to their

Landhold and in tribute to him, every year, they painted bright eggs with his arrows on them. Or so the legends said.

Marielle smiled wistfully, wondering if Tamerlan would confirm that story if she asked him. If he were alive at all. Her smile faded with the reminder.

"I'm not sure why you're smiling," Jhinn said grimly. "This next part is on you. You alone must find and steal this crown. I won't leave my boat again. And the guards were right. You look like a refugee."

She felt her face heat, almost snapping back that he looked no better, but she doubted he would care. His eyes were bright for the first time in days as they lighted on his people in family boats and gondolas throughout the city.

"You'll give them time to evacuate, right?" he asked, hope in his voice.

"The Waverunners?"

"Yes."

"So, you do care about *someone* even though you didn't care about my people."

He snorted. "Mine are alive."

She dropped her oar on the boat floor and strode over to him, leaning so her face was inches from his. "I think you should know better than that now, Jhinn. I think it's time that you recognize that the world might not be entirely what you thought it was."

"Don't think I haven't," he growled. "But now I have people to warn and you have a crown to find. I'll drop you off at that message tree." He pointed to a place where people were surrounding a tall pole, checking the pigeonholes surrounding it for messages and postings. "Meet me there again at this time tomorrow. And don't even think of freeing the city until then."

"I don't take orders from you, Jhinn," Marielle whispered.

His eyes narrowed. "I saved your life. I think you owe me something."

She swallowed. He was right. "Of course I'll give you time to save your people."

She scrambled out of the boat and onto the ledge of the canal, taking the small leather satchel she'd packed with her. There wasn't much in it beyond the letter from the Captain and Etienne's letter, but maybe that would get her the funds she needed to clean up. If everyone was watching her thinking that she was nothing more than a refugee, then it was going to be hard to get into the palace.

She climbed the stairs to the street above hurriedly, flinching against the smells bombarding her – mint and tarragon from the hanging herbs, the smell of eggs, and the heady cilantro scent of anticipation filled the streets.

In between that, the scents of the individual people and their problems poured over her. She was glad of it. Even this was better than the constant simmering scent of despair that had filled the gondola since Choan. Something familiar – a mandarin orange scent laced with rust made her nose wrinkle and then a hand settle on her arm.

"We need to stop meeting like this."

She turned to see Etienne and her mouth dropped open.

"How? What? How did you find me here? I just arrived!"

"I've been watching the gate," he said coolly. "This is the most logical entrance to the city if you're coming from Choan. Follow me. We shouldn't speak on the street."

She did follow him, but she didn't close her mouth behind the protective cover of the veil. How had he arrived before them? And why was he waiting for her? It was hard not to encourage a flicker of hope. Maybe she wouldn't have to do this alone. Maybe she'd have an ally with her.

The inn he took her to was close by, the doorframe draped with a dozen yellow ribbons and brightly painted eggs. Etienne strode past the muscled tough protecting the door and into a mostly empty common room. He nodded to the innkeeper who was polishing glasses behind a long bar.

"Extra if she's staying, too," the innkeeper said, not even looking up.

"She'll be in my room," Etienne said shortly.

"Still extra."

Etienne tossed him a coin with a sigh. The innkeeper caught it without looking up.

Etienne had all this planned out, it would seem. The inn. The meeting. He led her up the stair and opened the door to one of the rooms. On the bed, he'd spread out a clean set of trousers, boots, shirt, vest, scarf, and coat. They were clearly for her unless Etienne's figure and tastes had changed a lot in a matter of days. He'd planned this, too. She turned with a frown as he shut the door.

He raised a hand, forestalling her questions.

"Allegra is setting up a Xin in exile. Refugees from Choan have already joined her there. That's taken care of. The moment Xin lifted, I knew you'd need my help here. So don't be upset. I will rejoin her and very soon – I have not abandoned our plan."

"Of course," Marielle said warily, still confused by all the efficiency.

"I received word by pigeon as I traveled here that someone fulfilled the prophecy of the Son of Mer for the Retribution. It impressed them so much that they are returning home by sea to prepare their people for the coming of the Son of Mer."

"They are?" Marielle asked, gasping.

"Jhinn would only have walked on land if it was the only way," Etienne said calmly. "Which means we've lost Tamerlan somehow."

Marielle nodded mutely, her eyes tearing up. He'd figured all of that out just because the Retribution had left?

"Which means you need me to help you get in the palace in the way that Tamerlan might have. But I'd already anticipated that as soon as Xin lifted. You need me to help you identify the crown with Lila's avatar. You need me to provide money for the lodgings, food, and clothing that you need. So, I came."

He looked so serious.

She didn't care. She stumbled to him and wrapped him in a hug. He stiffened in her arms and she still didn't care. He'd thought about them! He'd realized she would need help, and that he couldn't do this alone and he'd helped!

"Was Allegra happy to see you when you woke up?" she asked as she pulled away.

He still looked stunned by her embrace and even more so by the question.

"What does that have to do with our goals?"

She laughed. He was so dense about anything that wasn't strictly logical and serious.

"Nothing. I just thought she might be happy to see you."

"She was relieved by the help I could provide with the evacuation and organizing the logistics of relocating an entire populace," Etienne agreed.

Marielle laughed. "I bet she wasn't happy when you chose to leave again."

Etienne shook his head as if she was being ridiculous. "I will go and fetch us dinner while you wash and dress. If we want to attempt entry to the palace tonight, our best chance will be if we are clean, well-dressed, and fed."

Marielle nodded, matching his serious with her own.

"Thank you, Etienne."

He nodded and left her to the room to dress with shaking hands. She was going to see her mother tonight. Somehow the thought of that made her more nervous than waking a dragon did, but Etienne had given her hope again. She was not alone.

21: DENIALS

It had been painful to ask Avandre to arrange a meeting for him with Variena. Painful because if Tamerlan hadn't ruined his plans months ago Yan would be in his hands right now, ruled by him, with people begging for audiences with him instead of the other way around. Humility was a painful dish to consume.

He schooled his face to politeness and followed the guards through the palace with Marielle at his side, disguising the way he still hunched over the pain in his healing abdomen. Allegra's cures were almost complete, but he still fought pain by the hour. Sometimes it took all his strength to hide the effort of masking it.

Marielle had her veil up – not, he suspected, because she needed it up but because she was anxious about this meeting. She shouldn't be. He wouldn't have set the meeting if he didn't think she could handle her mother. After all, she handled Tamerlan and he was far crazier than Variena. Probably.

Uncertainty was the luxury of the weak.

The palace was a ruin. Of course. A red door woman might be able to seduce the hearts and minds of a band of refugees, but that hardly qualified her to run a palace staff. Or a palace guard regiment, for that matter. He hadn't seen a guard here at the palace that he wouldn't have put on notice if they'd been in his palace at Jingen. The one leading them now had his swordbelt at a sloppy angle. His salute had barely sufficed. The guard he passed a moment ago smelled of alcohol and the guards at the gate had been missing their helms. It had taken all his self-control not to dress them down.

Allegra had at least been able to run a city with aplomb. He missed her efficiency. Her certainty. She was going to be furious with him when he returned, but he liked her furious. It went hand in hand with her ambition.

He smiled reassuringly at Marielle as she stiffened beside him.

"Not much further," he said in honeyed tones. But he felt tense like a spring under compression. The disrepair of the castle – the way it hadn't yet been patched, the rubble merely cleared away – was a bad sign. Where was Zi'fen? Variena might not know how to run a palace, but Decebel did. It worried him that the man's touch wasn't present here. It suggested there was something going on that he didn't know about. And that made him nervous.

Subtly, he touched the sword at his side and glanced at the one he'd given Marielle. They were armed. For all the good that would do if things went wrong. Almost, he wished for Tamerlan's unpredictability to unleash on this court. Almost.

If Marielle was to be believed, he was dead. But there were plenty of other hells he'd already survived. He may have survived the wrath of Jhinn as well. Maybe he'd even fled that dragon in time. He had the ability when he was possessed. Etienne had seen him move so fast you couldn't see the action.

Funny that Jhinn had been so quick to strike him down after everything Tamerlan had done when his pathetic boat was stuck in that fountain. But unfaithfulness was as predictable as Spring.

Spring. Which shouldn't be here for months – and yet it was. Even the weather was reacting to the calamities that had befallen them all. No, Etienne, this is not time for speculation. Keep yourself alert.

He purposely let his eyes note each cornice and column as they traveled through what had once been gleaming marble halls. If they'd come by water, they'd be in the Great Hall already. But they came, instead, by foot. And the guards had taken them to the Great Hall by the long way. Intentionally, he was sure. A show of force? A bit of drama? Or was there something they were meant to see on the journey? Maybe the disrepair was a ruse hiding something else?

Marielle cleared her throat behind her scarf, and he gave her a bland smile. She was needed for this – and not just because she was his only ally. No one else had a better chance of throwing Variena off her game than her daughter brought back from the dead.

He couldn't wait to see the woman's face. His lip twitched with eagerness.

The guard opened the last door – an ornate gilt-covered travesty with dents and chips where fighting had taken place in the revolt – and announced them into the huge nearly empty hall.

"The former Lord Mythos, Etienne Velendark and his companion."

Good. No mention of Marielle's name.

The guard withdrew and Etienne strode into the room, taking in the scene. She hadn't filled it with trinkets. That was a small note in her favor. In fact, she'd cleared out all the decoration and curiosities and left only a large ivory carved throne on a dais. Interesting.

She'd also opened the door to the dragon's wound and left it open.

An interesting choice. One that suited her violent nature and fuming resentment.

He could use that.

If he'd been anyone else, he might have been awed by her as she sat waiting for him on her throne. He might have been awed by her extravagant blue satin dress like a piece of night sky. She'd certainly kept the local dressmakers employed. It was garnished to an inch of its life. Exactly the dress a red door woman would wear to prove she wasn't that anymore, high collar and all.

"Variena," he said when he was only halfway to the throne. He could hear Marielle's boots behind him on the polished marble. "You kept at least part of the palace intact, I see."

"You will address me as Lady Legend," Variena said, tension ringing in her voice and he almost smiled. Point one to him.

On her head, sitting heavily in that dark curling hair, was the very crown they were looking for – a crown bedecked in diamonds and sapphires. How very Lila Cherrylocks. He recognized it from his reading and it brought a slight smile to his lips. Point two to him.

"Lady Legend," he said, drawing the name out to show her exactly how much he thought of it. "But where is your esteemed ally? Or has Zi'fen taken leave of you here to manage his own landhold?"

Marielle was beside him now and he felt her stiffen at his words.

A man he had thought was one of Variena's guards stepped out from the wall behind the throne.

"I am Daen Zi'fen," the man said.

Etienne didn't gasp like Marielle did, but he was surprised. The son. The eldest son, if he wasn't mistaken. Maybe fifteen years older than Tamerlan, but still young. The way he laid a hand familiarly over Variena's was interesting, though. He looked very like Tamerlan, though more smug, a lot more boring, less raw, less insane – that part wasn't difficult – there were people who foamed at the mouth who were more sane that Tamerlan.

"My pardon," Etienne said carefully. "I had expected *Decebal Zi'fen.*"

"Unfortunately," Variena said smoothly, "Decebel was killed in the fighting to take Yan. The former palace guard was shockingly tenacious."

Point one to Variena. There was no way Decebel had died by any hand but hers.

"Shocking," Etienne said, his eyes wandering to the glowing hole in the ground so very close to where they were. He could feel the power emanating from it. It called to him like wine to a drunk. And like the same drunk, he must keep that hidden. He let his gaze turn to the hand on Variena's throne. "How lucky you were to have made a new alliance with his son. Shall I assume a royal wedding is not far off?"

"Indeed," Variena's eyes narrowed in a shrewd way that belied the smug smile on her face. "And you've found a consort for yourself, as well. How fortunate."

The curiosity was killing her. Perfect.

He glanced at Marielle. The strip of face he could see was pale, and no wonder. Her mother had just confessed to killing the father of her brand new husband and taking his brother as her new fiancé. It was enough to shock anyone – and Marielle hated injustice. She must know her mother was wielding power like a cudgel.

"You keep the dragon's wound exposed?" he said, turning her question.

She frowned, watching him with speculation in her eyes. "It is an awful practice, sacrificing the daughters of the cities to the dragon, don't you think? I've chosen to sacrifice my enemies there instead. Hardly a sacrifice at all, if I'm honest. I keep it handy at these meetings, in case it is required."

Oh, clever. A nice glowing threat. Point two to Variena, but he was not done yet.

"And yet you were willing to take payment for the life of your own daughter. How ironic."

She hissed at his words and he smiled. Point three to Etienne.

"You still haven't introduced your companion," she said through gritted teeth.

"Haven't I? Well, speaking of children sold, may I present my companion," he said lifting a brow, his eyes lingering on the crown. "Who, I believe, you may already know. Marielle Velendark."

Marielle ripped off her scarf and now he couldn't hide his quick flash of a smile at the shock in Variena's eyes.

"But you're dead!" she said. And though she turned pale she made no move to stand or to embrace her daughter. She merely sat, idly holding the hand of Decebel's eldest son.

Cold, cold heart. He wouldn't have been troubled to steal from her no matter who she was. But if he'd had a conscience it certainly wouldn't bother him now.

"I'm alive, mother," Marielle said in a voice that hardly quavered. She'd grown in these last months. She was more than a match for her mother now. "We're here to warn you. Your city is about to fall. You must evacuate it immediately to save the lives of innocents."

And that was so very in character for her. Direct. To the point. Fair.

And completely unselfish.

No recriminations. No hurt that her mother had clearly severed all affection for her. He admired that. If things had been different, if he hadn't tried to sacrifice her himself, he might have been persuaded to love her – as much as he loved anyone.

He'd always found respect to be a greater motivator than love, anyway. He respected Allegra. And he respected Marielle. They'd both earned it in their own way. Grudgingly, he even respected Variena, but that was more the respect you gave the crocodile – the respect of staying out of the range of its bite.

"I will do no such thing," Variena said firmly. "The people here are mine. As is the city. Mine in loyalty. Bound to me by blood. The riches are ours. The surrounding Landholds are ours. The laws support us. The coffers are ours to spend. We will not leave just because a disgraced fool and a city watchdog come with wild imaginings. My city will not fall. It has never fallen to anyone but me."

"The dragon is going to rise," Marielle said, desperately. She cared so much. She even thought she could sway her mother – who clearly had no heart at all. "I've seen it happen four times now! Many will die – the innocent and the guilty alike! And the only way to save them is to flee this place!"

Variena laughed. "It's an inventive story. I'll give you that, Mythos." She spared him a knowing look. "And such a persuasive mouth you've put it in. Smoke, mirrors, and creativity. What a grand performance you've made. But look through that opening, daughter." She gestured to the tear in the dragon's scales through the door and Marielle flinched. Of course. The last time she'd seen a tear like that, he'd been about to slit her throat. "The dragon lives. And it is in our thrall just as always."

Variena's hand trailed up to her crown and she brushed it lightly with her fingertips – almost as if she knew what it was – that it was the one key they needed to raise this dragon.

"Not this time. Please, mother – "

"Don't 'please, mother' me!" Variena snapped. "You found a comfortable life in the Scenters while I had to slave away for you. You have no idea what that's like. How hard I've had to work. How much I've had to sacrifice. You have no idea and you still want me to give it all up! Ungrateful!"

Marielle flinched as if she'd been slapped but her expression hardened.

Etienne felt his heart harden even more. There was nothing that irritated him more than watching someone take out their frustrations at their own choices on someone else.

"If you don't listen," Marielle said, weariness in every word, "then many will die for no reason."

"You've gone mad, child. And you bore me," Variena said. She didn't look bored. The look in her eye was pure cruelty. "You will begone from here and I will not see you again. Same to you, Mythos. I'm done here. Unless you would like to sate the dragon?"

She raised an eyebrow. Point Variena. She'd won this round. Although in winning, she had lost everything.

"We will accept your offer to leave alive," he said with a sweepingly elegant bow. "In the spirit it was given."

Charm and a threat. It was always best when you could pair them.

But now came the next problem. How would he warn the citizenry of Yan to leave when their leader refused to help?

22: On the Wrong Foot

MARIELLE

She wet her face a second time with the cloth Etienne had offered her. She'd known she'd lost her mother when she saw the woman through Tamerlan's eyes as Variena and her allies took the city – but what she hadn't realized was that she'd lost not just her memory of a kind woman who raised her until she was eight, but also any shred of affection or loyalty that woman might have had for her.

"Surely," Etienne said from his chair beside the inn window, "you must have realized she was paid for your life."

"Yes," Marielle said. Her voice sounded hopeless even to her.

"So why did you expect loyalty now?"

"I guess I didn't really believe it. I mean, you were the one who was going to slit my throat, and now you are my most trusted ally."

"That's different." His words were kind despite their natural coldness. "You know that I always act for the good of my people – whatever that might be. Variena acts for the good of Variena. Her response today was predictable. What I hadn't bet on was the loss of Decebal. I thought to turn them against each other, but the son is a puppet to her whims. Almost, it makes me miss your mad husband. He, at least, had a spine."

Marielle hid her choking half-sob in the cloth at the words 'mad husband.' Oh Tamerlan, why did it have to end like that? When it had only just begun?

She felt his loss like her missing eye – no, worse! It ached and ached all the time and there was nothing she could do but go on without him.

"The problem now, is how to warn the people without the complicity of their leader," Etienne said, not noticing her emotional moment.

Marielle strangled her burst of grief, schooling her voice to calmness. "The problem now, is how to get that crown."

Etienne waved a hand dismissively. "You saw how she stroked it. She will keep it close. In her bedroom, most likely. All you have to do is break in during the night and steal it as she sleeps."

"All?" Could he really think that was no issue?

"Yes. You'll go in by the secret ways. I can draw you a map. All these palaces are laid out the same way with the tower in the center. And the personal rooms of the ruler have all manner of secret entrances and passageways. It will be easy. You *can* sneak, can't you?"

"I'm no Lila Cherrylocks," she said drily. If Tamerlan was here, he could do this.

"No, you plan to *end* Lila Cherrylocks," he said with a smile. At least someone found that part amusing instead of terrifying.

"If she catches me in her rooms …"

"Then you'll have to destroy the crown very quickly. Bring a hammer with you. A big one."

"Great advice."

He ignored her snapping tone. "My task is much harder. I have allies – friends who had meant to help me overtake the city. But many are likely dead or disenchanted with me since I failed them."

His forehead was lined, and his mouth screwed up as he thought.

"Use criminals," Marielle said.

He looked up at her. "For what?"

"To spread the word," Marielle said. It was a good idea. An idea only a criminal or a Watch Officer would think of. "There are thieves and smugglers all over the city. They'll have their own networks, their own ways of communicating. They'll have people in the guilds. Speak to the right one and word will spread like wildfire. Criminals are interested in their own self-preservation. As are the guilds. Let that work to your advantage."

"Clever, Marielle."

His smile warmed her. She kept her shaking hands hidden. Now that she'd seen her mother and been rejected, her body seemed to be letting out all that ridiculous hope it had been holding onto in the form of shaking hands and a pounding heart.

"And where would you go to find these criminals?"

"A fence." It was an easy answer. She'd dealt with enough thieves in her time in the watch. "Pretend you have a valuable piece to sell. Someone will bite. If you can manage to be more charming than you were with my mo – Variena – " she stumbled over the name, "then you might convince them to take you to someone more important. I could do that part, if you want to sneak into the palace."

She looked up, trying not to hope too hard. Good thing she hadn't set her heart on it. He was already shaking his head.

"No. Despite her words, if she finds you in her bedchamber, she will not kill you. And you have experience destroying avatars. On the other hand, your time in the Watch makes you ill-suited to speak with the criminal element."

"And your experience as the City ruler does?" she lifted an eyebrow.

"More than you'd ever believe. Government is filled with the worst kinds of villain. But I must do my task before you do yours. I need time to get the word out. Time for people to evacuate the city."

"We don't dare wait, Etienne. We need to destroy the avatar as soon as we possibly can," Marielle said.

"Why the hurry?" He shook his head. "When you were fighting for Tamerlan's sanity it made sense. But now, with him gone, what does it matter?"

"We don't know for sure that he is dead," Marielle said in a small voice. "And if he is not, then Ram the Hunter has him and Ram is determined to make as many avatars as he can."

He drummed his fingers on the side of his chair looking out the window.

"I thought this was all so manageable," he said, frustration in his tone. "If I just made the right choices."

"Me, too," Marielle agreed.

"If I just tried hard enough."

"It doesn't work like that, Etienne. We've been put in an impossible situation. Either people die now while we fix things, or they keep dying forever," she said fiercely. They'd battled over this before and they were so close to the end now.

And didn't she know sacrifice? Didn't the constant breathless ache in her chest remind her that she'd already lost Tamerlan one way or another and she couldn't even mourn or weep, she had to keep pressing on. She had to finish the job.

"What if there are more dragons than you know?" Etienne said. "What if after you release this one and the one over the sea there are more yet? Maybe there are some we don't know about."

Coldness filled her but she forced strength into her words. "I'll deal with that, if it's true. If I must be cold, I will be like the ice of the mountains. If I must be hard, I will be harder than stone. If I must breathe fire, I will be a dragon myself. But I will see this through. I've lost too much to do anything else. I've given too deeply. I've cut my own heart out and presented it on a platter. What more is there to do but follow through?"

He sighed, dropping his head into his hands. She'd never seen him like this. She'd seen him edgy and calculating. She'd seen him charming and powerful. She'd seen him brave and self-sacrificing. She'd never seen him defeated.

"Don't give up, Etienne." She crossed the room and put a hand on his trembling shoulder. "We are almost at the part where we need you most."

His scoffing laugh was so close to a sob that she couldn't say if it might be one after all. "And what part is that?"

Deep despair washed black through the room darkening everything, filling her senses with the scent of licorice.

"The part where you rebuild the Dragonblood Plains and make them better," she pled.

"From nothing. With everything we have stripped from us."

"Naked we are born into the world, and yet we grow into wondrous creatures capable of reshaping everything. So, we start naked again? Maybe in rebirth, there is hope. Maybe we can break old chains, make new and better laws. Carve out a new and better set of cities."

He looked up and she almost gasped at the tears washing down his cheeks. Etienne crying? Etienne emotional? But he was nodding, too.

"Not just anyone can do that, Marielle."

"Not just *anyone* will do it. You will do it."

He was still nodding.

"But only if you stop feeling sorry for yourself," Marielle said, crossing her arms firmly. "I need some sleep, but think about this, Etienne. The dragon in Yan is still bound. And you know how to access that magic. Maybe you can do something with that, hmm?"

"Yes.

She stumbled to the bed, too wrung from emotions to think about anything else and collapsed into it, asleep almost immediately. The last thing she heard was the door quietly shutting behind Etienne. He was off to find a fence, she was sure.

They had to keep hoping. They couldn't give up before the end.

23: Thievery and Destruction

"This way," Gansen said in a low whisper, leading her through the dark with his lantern held high. He was a head taller than Marielle and his shadow was long and narrow.

They were both moving more slowly than they'd prefer, their boots encased in flour sacks to muffle any sound they might make. Marielle's boots were so new they occasionally squeaked if she wasn't careful and any squeak might give them away. She took every step with care, holding her breath at the risk of a squeak.

Marielle followed him with her heart in her throat. She'd met him for the first time an hour ago when Etienne introduced them.

"Gansen is a loyal man," Etienne had said as if that was all there was to say. "He'll get you into the passages and as far as the door."

Gansen had nodded gravely. "I serve as a butler in the palace, miss. But before the fall of Jingen I was master of the Seven

Dragons Brewery, privileged to oversee all the vintages and brews acquired by the Lord Mythos."

"But can you sneak?" Marielle had asked nervously. His scent was so confident and when he looked at Etienne loyalty and dedication filled her nose with the scent of daisies.

That was enough for her.

Marielle hefted the heavy stone hammer she'd found earlier that day. For an actual stonemason, it wasn't that heavy, but it was more than adequate to crack or crush the gems of a crown. Hopefully, that would be enough. She'd brought a metal chisel, too, in case she had to split the metal band somehow. She'd never destroyed jewelry before. Hopefully, it wouldn't prove too difficult. The crown had been made of gold woven to look like vines with sapphire and diamond leaves. She thought that should make it easier to break it – but she wouldn't know until she tried.

Already, her hands were sweating and her mouth dry. The last time she'd gone against a Legend, things had not gone well. Anything could happen this time. And she didn't dare fail.

"We're at the stairs now," Gansen whispered back as he carefully set a foot on the ancient wooden stairs, testing his weight.

They were ahead of schedule, if Marielle's internal clock was correct. Now that they were actually here, she was finding it hard to concentrate. Three days, she'd waited while Etienne found allies in the criminal world of Yan. Three days while they did all they could to organize an evacuation of the common people. Three days while they roped Jhinn and his Waverunners into the mix. They'd taken as many people as they could out of the city already, hidden on boats. The canals of Yan were as empty as a fresh-dug grave. She'd heard complaining in the streets as people struggled to get around the city without their usual transportation.

And now it was time. As she snuck up the stairs, Etienne would be rallying the rest of the people he had warned. They'd be leaving the city in secret. And if their timing was perfect, then she should be at the door of Variena's room at the same time that he used the magic he managed to siphon from the sleeping dragon to create one final alert to the people of the city. It was the most they could do. It was their best effort. Marielle already knew it wouldn't be enough.

She felt for the sword at her side and the hammer in her hand. She was ready.

The stairs squeaked under her foot and they both froze for long minutes. Nothing else stirred the darkness except the rustling of mice. If anyone had heard them, they hadn't decided to act yet.

Marielle forced her feet to keep climbing and then to follow Gansen down the long, narrow corridor at the top of the steps. The dust was so thick that it puffed up with every step and even Gansen had wound a neck-scarf around his face so he wouldn't cough and sneeze.

"They're for emergencies," Etienne had told her. "Fires. Assassination attempts. Wars. Anything that might make a ruler need to flee."

"And no one used them during the uprising?" Marielle had pressed.

"They must not have had the chance. Which means that Variena probably doesn't know about them. The perfect weapon is the one that no one knows you have."

"But Gansen knows?"

"I gave him a map three days ago and he explored the tunnels. He'll lead you through to your mother's door," Etienne had assured her.

She hoped he was right.

"We're here," Gansen breathed, turning only his head to look at her as he leaned as far into the wall as he could so she could slip by.

She barely made it past him, even with her body shoved as far against her wall as she could get it, their bellies pressing together as she passed him.

She let out a long breath, checking to be sure she knew exactly where the latch on the secret door was before Gansen left with the lantern.

"Give me five minutes," he breathed.

He wanted a head start. And no wonder. He would barely have time to exit the city if she managed to wake the dragon. She reached into her pocket and carefully pulled out the small hourglass she'd brought. The last grains fell through the top bulb and she set it on the ground. She wouldn't need it now.

"Hurry," she whispered.

He nodded, his face serious. They'd told everyone that the dragon was going to rise. What they hadn't told them was that Marielle was the one who was going to release it.

She didn't hear his footfalls as he hurried away. Instead, she waited for the glow to disappear as she counted in her mind. Hopefully, she'd given him enough time. She set her hand on the latch and gripped the handle of the hammer harder, swallowing as she carefully slid the latch open and cracked the secret door slightly open. Soft light flooded into the secret passage and her breath caught in her lungs, but it wasn't a lantern or wall lamps. It was too faint for that. She eased the door open just a little more and slipped into the silent room.

The door came out in a sitting area, surrounded by books, disguised as one of the many bookcases. Etienne claimed she would come out into a "private study" attached to the bedroom. There were five rooms in the suite and though they both thought that Variena would keep the crown in her bedroom, it could be in any one of them. Or none of them.

Marielle slid the potato sacks off her boots – they were quiet but too bulky for this work – stashed them back into the passageway and wedged the door with a book. There was no way she was getting trapped in here with her traitorous mother. No way at all.

With a last steadying breath, she crept across the study. There were no drawers or trunks in the room. No place to hide a crown – especially not one as bulky as this with so many gems.

The next room was opulent, but also a poor bet. Plants and cages covered in heavy cloth filled the heavily ornamented room. Birds. Variena had always loved birds. They must sleep under the cloths. Marielle almost held her breath as she slipped through the room. If she made a wrong move. she'd wake them up and alert anyone. If the crown was inside one of the cages, she'd have to check here for it last of all.

There were two doors leading from here. One was larger and more ornate than the others. The way out to the halls beyond, if Marielle was any guess. The other was smaller – the bedroom, perhaps.

There was a sound coming from the next room. Her hand trembled as it rested on the doorknob and slowly turned it. It opened to reveal Variena, standing right in the doorway, one hand on her hip.

She barely managed to catch the scream in her throat at the sight of her mother. Variena was dressed like she was expecting company in a long satin nightdress of rich cherry red.

"Looking for this?" she asked, holding her crown up on a single finger as if it was worth nothing at all.

Marielle swallowed.

"Take it, if you must," her mother said with a sly smile.

Marielle hesitated. But after all, it was what she was here for. And her mother had just offered it to her. She snatched for it.

Before she could touch the crown, a hand caught her wrist. A hand in a heavy leather glove and bracer.

It pulled her through the door and flung her to the bed. She rolled across it, turning her momentum into motion and popping up on the other side of the bed on her feet, hammer at the ready.

"I told you she would come, Variena," Tamerlan said.

Icy cold flashed across Marielle followed immediately by a wave of fire.

He was alive!

Not sane, oh no, she could smell the insanity of Legend like she could smell an open cesspit, but he was alive. She could feel her heart melting even as she kept her guard up. It wasn't really Tamerlan – and yet – it was. He was in there somewhere. There was still hope for him!

The look on his face and the slight sway of his walk was almost identifiable.

"Lila?" she ventured.

Tamerlan's grin was not his own. It was fierce and crafty. It was matched almost identically by Variena's.

"Clever girl," he said.

She couldn't help the longing that surged through her like a summer storm. Maybe, when she destroyed the crown, she'd get him back. Even if it was just for a few moments.

"I told your dear mother that you would know me. Unlike you, she seems to understand what makes sense in this situation."

"I know that you're in there, Tamerlan," Marielle whispered, locking eyes with him. "Please be strong."

He'd said once that he thought she might have to kill him someday. She hadn't really thought he meant it. But perhaps he did. Perhaps that was better than dying a moment at a time as someone stole your body and will?

Variena cleared her throat. "I'm not ornamental here, love."

She shot a glance at Tamerlan.

"I haven't forgotten our bargain," Tamerlan said – or Lila, rather. "Get the ingredients I asked for, and I will make you an access to the Bridge of Legends. You will have power beyond your wildest dreams, only give the girl to me."

"And it will really work?" Variena's eyes shone with hunger and something lurched inside Marielle. It had been hard to believe that her mother would willingly sell her before – but it wasn't hard now. Not with Variena bargaining her price right here in the same room. She could smell the greed flowing from her, burning Marielle's nose like washing soda.

"It worked for this son of Decebel Zi'fen. You know the family. Watch me move and walk. Listen to me speak. You know this vessel is possessed by a Legend. This is no Zi'fen anymore. And you could have that power, too. You want more than this single city, don't you?" Lila practically purred. She kept her sword tip aimed toward Marielle, but she leaned intimately toward Variena with a small half-smile as she tried to lure her into freeing more Legends. "You want more than watching your back all the time, not trusting your allies or subordinates. You want a way to finally know that you are unshakable – untouchable. Trust me. I will give you that and more."

"She'll drive you insane," Marielle said, hammer still held out. "She'll take what's left of your life and ruin it."

"There's nothing here to ruin, girl," Variena said bitterly. She didn't even glance at Marielle. "What do you need, Legend?"

"Gather the spices and meet me in the Grand Hall," Lila said. "I'll deal with your daughter here and then come below and make you a Legend."

Variena's smile was cold and hard as glass. "Agreed."

"I'll take that," Lila said, snatching the crown from her hand. Variena hardly seemed to notice.

Marielle's stomach twisted at the cold look on her mother's face.

"Mother. Please."

Variena never once turned as she snatched a silken robe from a hook, wrapped it around herself and strode out of the room like a triumphant general.

"Please," Marielle whispered, but it was too late. Her mother had bargained with the devil and she'd lost for them all.

"A lovely woman, your mother. We could have been good friends," Lila purred. But Marielle saw a flicker behind those eyes. Was Tamerlan in there?

"Tamerlan, please," she begged.

"Be glad it is me that has you and not Ram the Hunter," Lila purred. "I'm not so cruel. He was right, it turns out that you must be made into an avatar. Oh, don't look at me like that. It wouldn't have come to this if you hadn't slain all of our friends. Or rivals. Or whatever they were. But we're running thin, now. We can't afford to lose anymore, and that means you need to be disposed of. And we have dragons to leash. Two birds and one stone and all that."

Lila tossed the crown in the air and caught it again.

"All the dragons that were leashed have flown now," Marielle said tightly. She was calculating how to throw the hammer at Tamerlan as her heart slowly shredded in her chest. She was going to have to hurt him – maim him – maybe even kill him. Could she do that? Her heart sped so fast at the thought of it that it made her thoughts stall and start again as her breath sped so quickly that she felt like she wasn't getting any air at all.

Inside, her heart felt hollow.

She weighed the hammer in her hands.

"Did you think they lay down quietly for us the first time? Of course not. The sacrifice comes first and then the dragon lies down and you can build on it. We moved the avatars to the cities after, of course. Mine was easiest to move."

She held the crown up with a smile, gazing at how it sparkled in the light. In that moment of distraction, Marielle threw the hammer.

It spun through the air, but Lila only laughed, snatching it out of the air even as it spun. Marielle didn't wait to see what she would do next. She needed to move while Lila was distracted. She drew her dagger and lunged forward all at once, dodging around the bed and trying to dodge around Lila.

Tamerlan's hand reached out and plucked her up into the air as easily as the other hand had plucked the spinning hammer from the air. He knocked the knife from her hand with one blow of the hammer, and drove her forward, slamming her down on the soft feather mattress of the bed, face first. She tried to sputter, but he held her tight to the bed with one hand as another worked on something. After a moment she felt her boot tugged off and something tied around her ankle. She tried to kick, but it cinched tight to one of the four posts of the bed.

He flipped her over and then deftly tied her other foot with one hand while he held her down despite all her thrashing. Had he always been so strong? When he was himself, he was nothing but gentle. He was like a songbird hopping along a rail, barely leaving a mark in the snow.

Lila caught her eye and laughed harshly. "He wastes this strength. What's the point of being powerful if you don't use it?"

"If you don't exploit people, you mean?" Marielle threw the words at her.

"If you don't lay waste to every enemy, plunder all their wealth and pluck their cities from their fingers like grapes from the vine." Her cruel smile twisted Tamerlan's face and then Lila pulled the crown from his wrist where it had been dangling like an over-large bracelet and jammed it over Marielle's head. "You can wear this while I kill you. Don't worry, I'll do it quickly and at least you'll have what you came for." Her grin widened. "See? I'm the merciful kind of villain."

"You don't have to be a villain," Marielle said through trembling lips. "You could be the hero of this story."

Lila laughed.

"Tamerlan believed that once and look where it brought him. We were always the villains, Marielle. We were villains since before we were Legends. It was only the wishes of storytellers and bards that ever made us seem like anything else. Isn't it funny? Like a little joke between you and me and Ram and Tamerlan? Because we're the only ones who know it. Your mother certainly doesn't. She's begging for the chance to be an avatar – if only a temporary one. But don't worry about that, either. Once she has a taste of us, she'll be so addicted to the magic that she won't stop. Just like Tamerlan. And we'll ruin her life just like we ruined his. We can call it your revenge if you think that will make you feel better. But before that, I'm going to make you an avatar and put you in one of those cages your mother keeps birds in. I think that feels fitting. In just a few hours, you'll be over the Bridge here with us. And maybe, if you're really lucky, you might see your Tamerlan again – in a mirror when you take over his body against his will."

Marielle thought she was going to be sick, as Lila fought her arms, forcing one into a loop she had ready in a length of silk. She caught Marielle's hand, cinching the tie in place.

"Please," Marielle begged. "Please, Tamerlan. If you ever loved me …"

There wasn't a shred of pity in her husband's eyes as he got the next rope ready. This wasn't working! She wasn't ready to die like this!

She had to think of something…

24: Crown

No rest. No sleep. No chance.

He'd hammered at mental walls until he couldn't fight anymore.

He'd tried to stop looking, but his eyes never closed.

He'd prayed to any god he remembered.

He wished – more than anything – that he'd begged Marielle to kill him while she still could. Or Jhinn. Or Etienne.

If he had his own hands available, he'd do it himself. Without regrets.

If only Jhinn had hit harder, he might have killed Tamerlan. Why hadn't he hit harder?

But there was no room for resentment in this pool of living despair. There was no room for rage. No room for agony. Only desperate, swirling, unending despair forever and ever eating his soul from the inside like a cancer.

He couldn't even breathe on his own – couldn't even suck in sweet oxygen. Couldn't stop Ram or Lila when they pushed his body far past the limit. Not when Ram jumped from the tail of the dragon while it swooped low, falling nearly a hundred paces into the river. Not when they refused to let him sleep, merely switching off who had control of him while the other rested, pushing his body in an endless roil of motion.

None of that was anything compared to this. It was a sweet kiss of life compared to the feeling in his heart when Marielle stepped into the room. It was the warm summer breeze compared to how his heart broke when his hands caught her and held her, when they tied her up like an animal, when his ears ignored her pleas and his lips – traitorous lips! – formed a cruel smile.

He tried to scream from within, but no sound came. He pounded and battered against walls too high now to penetrate. Lila and Ram had learned from the past. They'd learned how to keep their focus perfect so there was never a crack to exploit.

He grabbed Marielle's arm, fitting the loop over it and tying it while his other arm kept her pinned. He was howling inside.

Let me out, Lila! Let me out!

She would pay for this! They all would pay!

They'd stopped talking to him now that they had his body to use. Stopped even acknowledging that he'd ever been there. Maybe his soul was gone, and he just didn't know it.

There was no hope of ever escaping them, and yet he pounded and battered. Not this! Please, not this!

Marielle caught his eye and his heart broke at the depths of her deep, purple eyes. She was so vulnerable. So fragile. And he was going to murder her with his own hands – heart of his heart, life of his life.

His soul felt like it was ripping in half.

And then, her unbound hand moved like a snake in a direction Lila hadn't anticipated, wrenching the crown from her head and flinging it against the stone wall. It hit with a clatter, one of the gemstones flying off and tumbling across the thick rugs piled on the bedroom floor.

Lila spun toward the wall, heart in her throat. There was a crack as her fear surged. Tamerlan pushed against the crack with all his might, flexing, shoving …

And like pushing through a stone wall that seems impenetrable but then crumbles, he went surging in, his mind taking over his body and shoving Lila aside.

"Marielle," he gasped, his lower lip quivering as he sucked in a sweet breath. He leaned in, stealing a fierce kiss. But there was no time to savor it. Hurriedly, his hands fumbled at her ties.

"Is that actually you?" she asked, tentative, afraid.

Lila and Ram were both battering at his mind. He clenched his teeth against them and shoved the barriers up as hard and strong as he could. It wouldn't be enough – but perhaps it could be for just long enough.

"It's me, Marielle, my sweet love. Oh, heart of my heart. Life of my life." He had her other arm free. He hurried down the bed, tearing at the binding around her foot. Kissing her ankle as he worked, her foot, her calf, anything, everything. "I'm here for now, but you must bind me. As soon as we get you free."

There. Her foot was free. He tore at the binding on the other foot as Ram and Lila bashed at his inner walls. He could feel them weakening.

"Marielle, I'm so sorry." He was babbling and he knew it, but he couldn't stop it. "I'm sorry that I almost killed you. I'm sorry that all this burden is on you. I should have been there to bear it with you."

"Tamerlan, it's okay. It's all okay."

"It's not. I can never make up for it." His hands were shaking. He drew his sword and flung it away and then leaned in to tear his lips across hers, to taste her sweet lips one more time. Oh, she was sweet, she was life. One last kiss, fiery and filled with every desperate hope he'd ever had that wouldn't come true. "You have to bind me. No. You have to *kill* me – as quickly as possible. Before any of this can get worse."

"I'm not going to kill you," she was half-sobbing as she said it. Somehow, she was in his arms, sweet softness and the scent of flowers and woman. She melted him from the spine outward. Her breath was soft on his face as she cupped it in her hands and whispered. "I love you, Tamerlan, I love you. I thought I'd lost you. Oh, sweet dragons, I'm happy to see you. Please, please be sane."

He wanted to relax into her arms and just let her take his despair for a moment, but there was no time. Even as she covered his face and neck in frantic kisses, he could feel Ram nearly breaching his walls.

He had to give her something. Something before he was gone forever. He held her tenderly, tucking his head down to kiss her as thoroughly as he could – one last gift – before begging her.

"Please, Marielle." They were both kneeling in a mess of bedcovers. His words came out in a frantic rush. "Please, you must tie me up. Indulge me in this one thing. I'm nearly gone again, and I don't want your death on my hands. Please!"

She nodded determinedly, grabbing the silken belts and making quick work of binding his hands. He breathed a sigh of relief. Her knots were tight and firm.

"Tie me to the bed. I don't dare underestimate them."

She nodded and complied, but the look on her face as like a shipwrecked sailor who had spotted land. She couldn't tear her eyes from him.

"I love you, Marielle," he said gently. "Please don't forget that."

"I won't," her voice broke as she tied her last knot.

"And now, my sweet wife," he said, trying to convey with a smile all his affection and loyalty in a single look. "And now, comes the time where you must end me. In a moment, you will hammer that crown to smithereens, and Lila will be gone, and the dragon will rise – just as you and I hope. And when that happens, I won't be able to keep Ram away. And he will take me over for the rest of my life. And it will be no life. If he can, he will do worse things to you than Lila ever would. Please, do this for me, Marielle. One last mercy. One last gift."

Marielle's face hardened. Good. She was ready.

"Thank you," he breathed.

But she leapt from the bed, her good eye full of fire, snatched up the hammer and ran across the room to where the crown lay on the ground. She fell to her knees and began to pound it, both hands swinging the hammer as hard as she could.

With every strike, he felt Lila clawing at his mind. He was screaming before he realized it, but when he tried to stop, he bit his tongue, tasting blood.

Pain flashed across his vision, but he held on as he watched Marielle. She was glorious. Like a winter storm come alive, her hair untangled from her braid, flying as she battered the crown with her hammer, chunks of gemstone flying out and slicing her cheeks and hands with every stroke. It was nothing now but broken gems and battered metal and then a black liquid like ink spilled out and as Marielle scrambled back, it rose up into the air like smoke, forming the shape of a curvaceous, winking woman with a long red braid and then bursting in a shower of rubies.

Red gemstones flew in every direction, scoring his skin with painful trails and spattering across the bed and floor like a stone firework.

He felt Lila scream out of existence and then Ram seemed to grow, his fists battering Tamerlan's walls. He couldn't be stronger if he was the dragon under their feet, bucking as it awoke.

Marielle looked to him, gasping in huge breaths, her eyes shining in triumph.

She'd done it.

Her face broke into a smile – the most beautiful thing he'd ever seen and he smiled with her.

He could feel Ram breaching his walls. There was no time left to beg her to kill him. He settled for mouthing the words, "I love you."

Ram stole his body, wresting it from his grip and sending him to his knees in a howl of agony as the Legend took him again.

25: FLIGHT OF YAN

She'd done it! She'd destroyed the avatar!

Her eyes sought Tamerlan's sharing this intense moment of victory with him. His smile was like the rays of the sun at noon, blinding her. There had to be hope for him. With a smile like that – a love like that. She was right not to kill him. She was right –

He howled like a soul in hell, falling to his knees as the dragon began to buck underneath them.

Stop, Yan! Please lie still! She tried to tell the dragon with her mind. She'd spoken to the others. Why did he feel so far away?

Was it you who woke me?

Tamerlan's howl continued and she took a step toward him and then froze. Should she help him? Or should she stay back? What if Ram the Hunter had him already? Her heart froze in her chest. She couldn't do what he asked. She just couldn't. Not even with a Legend looking at her through his eyes.

It was me, she said to the dragon. Can you lie still while people flee your back?

Why?

Tamerlan stopped screaming, his head whipping up and the calculating look on his face not his at all. She held the hammer up, wishing she'd tied him to the bed like Lila had been trying to tie her.

She had to focus on Yan. Or people were going to die.

I need them to be free, she said in her mind. Just like I am trying to free all of your kind. If you can just wait a few hours —

All of my kind?

I think there's only one left. Across the ocean.

And you will free her?

It's what I'm planning.

Then we will go there now. I will take you.

No, please listen! I need you to wait! Just until the city on your back is clear of humans!

I will try to stay level and keep the humans on my back.

It doesn't work that way! Please!

The ground beneath her feet shifted and she was flung back against the wall. Ram the Hunter in Tamerlan's body growled at her.

Swallowing, she clung to the wall, pulling herself back to her feet. She needed a plan to keep him here. Maybe there was a way to lock him in the room. Carefully, she slid over the bed, keeping out of his reach as he growled at her.

"Stay, woman," he snarled. "If you leave, you'll always be looking for the knife in your back. You'll live your whole life knowing I can destroy you at any moment."

She ducked around him, barely avoiding his reach as she rushed through the door and slammed it behind her. There was a lock but no key. Frantically, she searched the room of cages, ripping their covers off their cages to an uproar of squawks and shrieks.

They were only birds. Gorgeous birds of every color and variation she could imagine – but only birds.

And no keys hung in their cages. But this time, when she left that room, she didn't go to the study, she went into another room – one with a balcony and a large window open to the city below and fancy, stuffed chair for guests to sit and talk. From here, in one of the palace towers, she watched as the tip of a wing rose up from the mud, water rolling off of it in the moonlight.

She clenched her jaw as she thought furiously.

Please, Yan, don't move. Please, wait for people to leave!

She heard a whisper in her ears coming in from the window. She ran to it and in the air, she heard Etienne's voice slipping through the breeze. It was his warning. The warning that was meant to go out to the whole city from the time she'd opened that door into the study until now.

"Flee the city while you can! Flee before the dragon rises! Flee!"

As soon as it was done the sound of bells ringing filled the air as every bell in the city began to ring at once. She stumbled back from the window. The position of the moon was changing.

I am rising. See how I can bear a city on my back? I will deliver you all to my sister dragon Xytexyx and you will free her as you have promised.

Marielle made a frustrated sound in her throat. Couldn't he wait just a few hours? She needed to secure Tamerlan and make sure the rest of the populace had fled!

You will flee, too. No, I will bear you there immediately.

Over the ocean? She didn't even know the way. She cursed mentally. Why did he have to be so difficult?

Why are you the one being so difficult? I can find others of my kind. You will wait patiently in this city.

Stupid dragon!

She spun at the sound of footsteps on the marble. Variena froze in the doorway, still in her robe, her eyes wide at the sight of Marielle.

"You!" Marielle snarled, feeling like all her frustration was focused on a single target.

The world tilted under her, but she kept her feet. This wasn't the first time she'd flown in a city attached to the back of a dragon. As soon as the floor stopped moving, she drew her sword.

"Where is he?" Variena asked, drawing herself up to her full height.

"In your bedroom," Marielle said, her mouth twisting as she spoke. "Do you have a key for the lock?"

A calculating look filled her mother's eyes. "I see you bested the man, child. You take after your mother."

"Do I?" It was all Marielle could do not to spit. Took after Variena? Was Variena kidding?

Crashes and shouts sounded in the background. Not everyone had made it out of the city – of course.

Marielle reined in her temper. Fury at her mother would have to wait. People were dying out there and they'd continue to die if they weren't helped.

"Mother," she said, keeping the venom out of her tone. "The dragon has risen, and he is planning to fly across the sea."

"You can't know that." Variena crossed her arms, defensively.

"And many of your people were unable to flee." It was all she could do not to glance to the window. "They need leadership. If they can find sheltered places – in the cellars or under bridges – anywhere that will protect them from falling buildings – then they need to get to them immediately."

"I'll do all of that once I have what the Legend promised me," Variena said with a shrug.

"I can't let you near him." Marielle lifted the sword's tip. It was only a pace away from her mother's chest. Could she strike if she had to? She shook her head, her hands suddenly shaking at the thought as memories of Variena flooded her mind. Variena hugging her close when she wept as a small child. Variena feeding her sweets and telling her she was a good girl. Her sword wavered.

"You won't hurt me," Variena scoffed, striding past Marielle with a look of disdain.

"Wait!" Marielle called. Her hands were shaking, but she couldn't let Variena free Tamerlan. She didn't dare. "It's not the same Legend that it was before. This one will tear you to pieces. You can't go in there!"

Variena's mouth twisted. "What are you going to do? Run me through with that sword just for looking at a man in my bedroom? Could you live with yourself if you did that?"

She'd won already. Marielle knew it from the sour taste on her tongue and she confirmed it by the scent of smugness rolling off Variena. Not regret for hurting her daughter. Just victory and pride.

"You're my mother," she pled, feeling foolish. What was she? Six years old again?

"Which is why you won't hurt me," Variena said with a scoffing smile.

Marielle cleared her throat, pushing back the tears that welled up. "So why are you so intent on hurting *me*? Won't you trust me in this one thing? I'm only asking you to do what is best for you, too."

Variena gave her a pitying look. "One day you'll understand, child, that a woman has very few options when it comes to embracing power and a seat at the tables of men. When your chance comes, you have to take it. No matter what it costs. There are plenty of red door women who gave everything up to raise children, taking jobs as washerwomen and maids. Horrible, work-filled lives. They were wrinkled and worn before they were forty and died shortly after that. I gave you to the Scenters for a better future – not just for you, but for me, too. And I'd do it again. Just like I'll sell your future if it's all I have to get one for myself. No one hands you anything in life, Marielle. You only get what you take. And if you were any good at this, you'd already know that and be takin as much as you could from *me*." She paused, considering. "This can be a lesson for you. Learn to be a strong woman and stop letting mindless compassion rule you. Stop being one of those stupid women who scrub clothes until they die."

She spun on her heel and strode through the door into the room of cages and a moment later, Marielle heard the latch of the door to the bedroom open. Betrayal welled up in her like a tide and she laughed at herself – a terrible bitter laugh. Why did she expect anything else? Variena had betrayed her again and again. Why did she think this would be any different?

She looked to the door where Variena had gone and back to the one she'd come through.

Marielle needed to meet back with Etienne at the rendezvous point. But if she left Variena with Tamerlan –

Her mother's scream pierced the air before she'd made a decision. She leapt for the doorway, dodging through the room of golden cages as the birds screamed their defiance, and bursting into the bedroom beyond. She made it just in time to see Tamerlan break her mother's neck with his freshly freed hands.

She never should have hesitated. She should have killed him like he'd asked.

She didn't hesitate now. She lunged with the sword, plunging it into his thigh, and darting back to lunge a second time. She had it through his ribs before he could drop Variena. The look of shock on his face nearly ruined her.

She didn't dare stop. She lunged again, but he grabbed the sword by the blade, not even noticing as it shredded his own palm when he ripped it from her grasp.

She was no fool. She turned and ran, pelting through the room of birds, her boots loud on the dressed stone floor. Feathers and shrieks filled the air as she fled into the study, slamming the door behind her. There was no lock. She ran to the bookcase, snatching up the book that wedged the door open.

Tamerlan burst into the study with a roar.

Marielle couldn't help the scream that tore from her lips as she ran into the secret passageway, pulling up her scarf as she sped through the thick dust, kicking up clouds of it all around her in the dark. She couldn't see a thing. The stairs would be coming up soon and she'd fall right down –

The ground bucked and she was thrown through the air.

Ooops. That's quite the current in the air over the ocean. Pleasant, but a touch turbulent.

She didn't know what 'turbulent' meant and she didn't care. She was tumbling down the stairs, hard wood hitting her shoulder, her knee, her ribs, her back.

"Ooof," the breath knocked out of her when she slammed into the floor at the bottom of the steps, cracking her chin so hard that she tasted blood.

She rolled immediately, stumbling blearily to her feet and fighting them as they tried to pull her into two separate directions. She could hear feet on the wooden stairs, descending.

Come on, Marielle!

She skidded along the hallway, coughing and choking on dust and blood.

The sound of the footsteps had changed. He was at the bottom.

She slammed into a wall and bounced off, gasping for breath.

A faint light was ahead. She sped toward it, almost able to make out where her path was now.

It was growing brighter. Her breath was loud in her ears, gasping and choking. She was almost there. What was going on? Why was there a lit lantern on the floor at the crossroads of two passages? She slowed, running past it and then stopping. She didn't remember which way to go. A hand reached out and pulled her into the shadows while another wrapped around her mouth. She bit back a scream and then she was shoved further into the shadows as the body of her kidnapper blocked her from the light.

She heard Tamerlan's footsteps slowing.

Her attacker struck him with something before Marielle realized what was in his hand.

Tamerlan fell like a piece of one of the crumbling buildings on the back of the dragon.

"Nothing seems to be going as planned," Etienne said wryly, stepping into the light. He was carrying a heavy iron chain that he'd hit Tamerlan with, and he hunched over slightly, his eyes tearing in the corners as if he were fighting a pain she couldn't see. He kneeled on the fallen man, wrapping the chain roughly around his arms and torso. "I'm guessing you didn't plan to stab him in the leg and belly, did you, Marielle?"

"I did not," Marielle said softly. "But I had to."

"Any idea where the dragon is flying to?" His voice was tense.

"*Xytexyx.*"

"Then I guess we'll ride this out and hope that we survive it – again."

26: THREE DAYS

Three days passed as slowly as a year anywhere else. Three days of hiding in cellars and under bridges. Three days were every face he saw was a living reminder of his failure. If he'd been better, more would have lived. If he'd been smarter, he would have found a way.

They'd managed to get all of the poor out of the city – surprisingly. All of the guilds, too. Etienne had been surprised by the power of the guilds to organize, but even more surprised by the sway the criminal groups had over the common folk. If he lived to rule again, he would remember that.

Which left many of the wealthy behind. But there were still innocents among them. Women and children who had not fled. And he felt every pair of their eyes on him as he went throughout the city explaining to them what had happened and what to expect.

He felt that almost as much as he felt the presence of Tamerlan – even though the man was unconscious – every time he came to visit Marielle where she hid under the palace bridge. She'd picked the place so she could be close to Jhinn. Who would have thought the boy would be stupid enough to ride a dragon a second time in a boat?

He'd dammed the moat in preparation for it when he could have been ferrying more people out of the city. It was hard for Etienne not to question him about why he thought that was best, but every time he opened his mouth, he remembered that it was his own failing that had brought them here. If only he'd been smarter, he could have found a way to make them listen. If only Marielle hadn't been in such a hurry … though when he heard her story of how close it had come to her mother becoming a second addict to that woeful spice, he couldn't blame her.

He snorted. They must be getting close, but it was hard to find a vantage point in the city safe enough to climb up and see the horizon. The dragon had been careful enough in his flight that most of the buildings were still standing – though all were crumbling.

Etienne had climbed up the central tower of the city twice – a process that left him trembling and weak with terror as it swayed wildly back and forth like a palm tree in a storm – and both times he'd seen only ocean, but the last time had been yesterday. Maybe they were closer now.

He felt a shift under his feet, almost as if the dragon had heard him, and he hurried to the nearest wall to hold on tight as the city slanted to the right. The streets went from horizontal to nearly vertical.

There was the view he'd been wanting. Now, he was cursing himself for wanting it. He slid into the nearby alley, barely avoiding carts tumbling down the streets and barrels rolling after them. He'd seen enough in that single glimpse – a white sprawling city on high rocks beside an ocean so blue it made the sky look pale. The green plants surrounding it on the other side were brighter than any he'd seen before. These were not the Dragonblood Plains. It didn't even seem like the same world, the colors were so brilliant.

He nodded his head as he clung to the wall of the building in the safety of the alley. They'd made it. Now, they just had to survive the landing.

27: LANDFALL

Jhinn watched Marielle carefully spooning broth into Tamerlan's lips. He swallowed it, though he murmured something unintelligible as he did it, banging his skull against the pillow she'd put between it and the stone. He did that all day long now.

There'd been fighting on the first day when he thrashed against the chains so hard that he fell in the canal and Marielle and Jhinn had to use all their strength to pull him back up to the ledge. It had been Tamerlan who had surfaced after that. And he'd begged them to push him back in the water. Begged them with tears in his eyes. Marielle had refused. And she'd pulled her knife when Jhinn tried to do what Tamerlan asked.

Which made him her enemy now, though the woman hardly seemed to know how to treat enemies. She guarded Tamerlan like a duck with one duckling. Feeding him, wrapping him in blankets, bathing his face with a damp cloth. Even when he was conscious and raving about how he would disembowel her and fill her with ungodly magic to harness the dragons and force them to the earth, she tended him. Even when he surfaced again as Tamerlan weeping and begging for death – when he made sense at all – she comforted him.

Sometimes, Jhinn didn't know whether Tamerlan was the crazy one, or Marielle.

Or Jhinn, for that matter.

Because he kept hearing that stupid prophecy in his head over and over again, and that was not the way a sane man thought.

He will open the Bridge and in that day, it is only the Heir of Mer who may close it again. In retribution, the heir of Queen Mer will lay waste to the Legends and return the dragons to their place and they will be quelled forever, their fury kept at bay for all eternity. In that day the landless will walk on Land and will be called the Son of Mer. In his unfaithfulness, he will be faithful. In his damnation, he will bring salvation to all.

In his unfaithfulness, he will be faithful. In his damnation he will bring salvation to all.

That was him. The unfaithful. The damned. And yet … if he could really believe this, if he could believe that the burden he'd taken on had been for everyone and that it had been what was needed to save them. If he could believe it, it would change everything.

He'd believed it in the moment that he'd done it. But now, he couldn't shake the feeling that he'd betrayed everything he ever was, and it felt like rot in his mouth and weakness in his bones.

He'd been thinking about the prophecy as he tried to puzzle it out over the days that he warned the people and then sat here with craven Marielle and her even more insane husband.

Was the heir of Queen Mer the same as the Son of Mer? What if they were two people? And the more he thought about it, the more he thought that was the right way to read that. Otherwise, why change the wording? Why not make it 'son' or 'heir' all the way through?

What if Marielle was the heir of Queen Mer? Queen Mer had been a common woman obsessed with saving a people. Wasn't that just like Marielle? Queen Mer had given them law and hope. Just like Marielle. And Marielle was the one slaying the avatars and returning the dragons to their place. It just seemed right.

Which only left two questions.

How was Marielle going to close the Bridge of Legends?

And was Jhinn the Son of Mer? After all, he'd saved Marielle so she could finish her work. Could that mean that he had been faithful in his unfaithfulness like the prophecy said, or was he just grasping at straws as he desperately hoped there would be redemption for him?

But these thoughts had softened him.

He didn't hate Marielle anymore.

But he did worry about her.

Because the more he thought about it, the more he was certain that the only way they could ever close the Bridge of Legends would be with the death of Tamerlan. And though he'd promised his friend he'd never let him stop them from accomplishing this, he had to admit that he wasn't ready to kill an innocent man for no other reason than that demons had broken his mind and taken his body.

He swallowed and watched Marielle as she sang a sweet song to Tamerlan – a child's song, he thought, while the man jerked and twitched against the metal chains Etienne had wrapped all around his body.

The world tilted, suddenly, and Jhinn was swept out of view of Marielle and Tamerlan as he fought his gondola.

Stay upright! Stay upright!

Oar in hand he plunged it into the water, pulling against the force of the sudden shift as his boat nearly collided with the wall. He pulled them back, paddling furiously. No damage.

He breathed out a sigh of relief as the water slid back again. It hadn't breached the dam, though it was still all gathered up along one side of the canal while the other side rose above the water, showing a waterline so ancient that it was thick with brown and black scum.

The dragon was descending. Wherever he landed, Jhinn hoped there was water. He might be slowly making peace with his unfaithfulness – might be clutching at straws of hope that there could be redemption for him in the results of it – but he wasn't ready to ever do it again.

He swallowed as the ground under them hit something hard and everything shivered causing masonry and dust to fill the air as it fell around them. His belly ached from worrying so hard. He glanced at Marielle and worry met worry in their gazes.

There was only one dragon left to free, but this one was going to be the toughest of all.

28: The Other Side of the Ocean

She ripped her eyes away from Jhinn and back to where Tamerlan muttered on the ledge beside the canal.

"Dragons," he said in a pained voice. "Too many. Too far."

"It's okay," she said, wiping his brow with the damp cloth. "Just rest."

But none of this was okay and it hadn't been okay for days. He was still in there somewhere, she thought, but whatever war was raging between Tamerlan and Ram in his mind had destroyed them both. Sometimes she didn't even know which of them was muttering to her. She didn't even bother to beg Etienne not to chain Tamerlan. She didn't know if it was a mercy that he was bound. Perhaps it actually saved him from the horrors he would otherwise be unleashing on the earth.

She'd tended his wounds, of course. The one on the thigh wasn't bad. She'd stitched it and she changed the bandages as often as she could – but the place where she'd stabbed him between the ribs was festering and no amount of cleaning had brought the infection down. Even if he hadn't been chained, she doubted he'd be going far with such a mortal injury.

She swallowed as she bathed his hot forehead. Tamerlan might be dying slowly despite her best efforts to keep him alive. She tried not to think about that. Tried instead, to focus on what was right in front of her.

They'd landed. Somewhere. And she would have to find the dragon now. She could smell Jhinn's trepidation mixing with his constant stream of guilt.

What was she going to do with Tamerlan while she went looking for Xytexyx?

You won't have far to go.

She gasped at Yan's voice in her mind. He'd stopped speaking to her after he lifted off from the ground on the Dragonblood Plains.

I have landed beside Xytexyx, the canals on my back flowing into the canals coming from hers. But we are too late.

Too late?

This dragon died many years ago. I mourn her loss.

Then … were they all free?

I think not. I sense another … somewhere.

Marielle let out a moan of despair. This was what she'd been holding onto. In all the desperation, all the misery, all the heartbreak she'd been telling herself that she was almost there. And she'd been lying to herself. She was not almost there. They were going to have to track down some mystery dragon. With Tamerlan delirious and possessed and insane. With Jhinn slowly bleeding out guilt and with her bearing such scars inside that she had to keep busy every minute of the day just to keep the pain away.

She couldn't do it.

She couldn't do even one more thing.

This was the end. Not because she'd lost, but because she just couldn't carry on.

The sound of lapping water made her look up and she gasped at how close Jhinn's gondola was. His face was only an arm-length away from hers.

"It is only the heir of Mer who can close it again," he said gently. "That's you, Marielle. We need you. Please don't give up."

"You don't understand," she whispered, putting her weary head in her hands. "The dragon here is dead. But we aren't free. Yan senses another somewhere."

"We'll find it."

"It could be anywhere," she protested. She felt like there were glass shards in her chest, cutting her with every breath, tearing her apart with any movement at all. "Anywhere. We'll never find it in time."

"In time for what?"

"To save Tamerlan! To free your people. To do what we promised to do."

Jhinn was silent for a long time.

"Marielle, we can only do what we can. But I think you can go a little further. Maybe just for today. And then you can think about it again tomorrow. Can you keep going for today, Marielle?"

Could she? She felt like she couldn't keep going *at all*. But she pulled her head from her hands and stood up. She'd gotten that far. Could she go just a little further?

She looked down at Tamerlan, chained and delirious and her lower lip began to tremble. She had to try. For him. For them all.

"Can you help me get him into the boat?" Jhinn asked. "You can't carry him, and I don't think he can walk."

Marielle nodded and focused on the work of lifting, rolling and dragging Tamerlan into the gondola. When they were done, she leaned against him, hugging him as she gasped for breath. He was heavy. And so were the chains binding him.

"The dragon says he lined up our canals with the canals of Xytexyx. If we let the water out of the dam in a waterway with a straight shot downhill, we have a good chance of reaching their river, and getting into Xytexyx."

Jhinn nodded soberly as she climbed into the gondola and kicked off from the canal ledge.

She just had to keep on going and keep on breathing. One step at a time.

They would find the other dragon. They would figure out how to destroy Ram's avatar – wherever it was. They would take it one step at a time. The first step, was tearing apart the dam. And she could do that. She just had to keep on hoping, keep on pushing forward, keep on refusing to allow anything else to thwart her will.

A pain blossomed in her chest – dull and soft, but aching – right over the Windrose.

Perfect timing.

She groaned.

29: Fevers and Nightmares

Nightmares filled his mind. He was Ram the Hunter, carefully trapping the last of the beasts – the one that had already fled to the other side of the world. He was laying a trap for it on the rocks beside the sea.

He was Tamerlan, carefully compounding a tincture. He weighed his sulfur carefully on a pair of brass scales.

He was a dragon, sleeping. Pain was all he could feel, his eyes sealed shut, his wings and legs held tightly in place.

He gasped. Marielle's face swam into view. She was wiping his brow, adjusting his eyepatch. Oh, Marielle. She was so gloriously beautiful in the sunlight. He'd never before had a person he knew he could trust absolutely, like he trusted Marielle. She would always do what was right. Always. And when the time came, she would slay him.

A wave of pain blossomed in his side – old pain. Pain he'd been living and breathing in constantly, he tried to adjust to ease it, but his arms were pinned by heavy chains.

Good.

Why was that good? He couldn't remember.

You're a fool.

He was a fool. He remembered that.

She doesn't love you.

That was for the best. He didn't want to hurt her. He wanted her to go on and live her life and be all the beautiful things he knew she would be. Someone's wife. Someone's mother. Someone's friend. Someone's protector, striding through the streets like the hammer of the Legends.

He could feel the smile on his lips.

Someone who isn't you.

Good. That was good, too.

And then the blackness took him, and he was Ram again.

I will kill her. I will kill them all.

Good. Good.

The dragons will pay.

I will make them pay in pain forever.

He was a dragon.

He was paying in pain.

30: Into Xytexyx

If she had to guess, she wouldn't have expected that the people on the other side of the ocean celebrated Springhatch, and yet their decorations put the Dragonblood Plains to shame.

As the gondola shot out of Xytexyx into the mouth of the river, where it flowed into the sea, they could see the grand city of Xytexyx ahead of them, rising up on the edge of the sea cliffs in glorious beauty. Every surface of the rocks was coated in thick green vegetation, and every rock towered above the sea as if the sea had slowly slipped lower, but the rock had remained firm and unmovable.

A fleet of ships were anchored just out from the river mouth and boats filled the river and the open bay – fishing boats, trading boats, passenger dinghies, and wide river boats. There were no family boats, though there were sleek gondolas in the river, filled to almost overflowing with people.

"There's the military forming up the shore," Etienne said sharply, pointing to where men and women thickly covered in tattoos rushed out of stubby passenger boats and onto the land, harpoons in hand. Each group of about fifty was led by a single Ki'Squall and all of their eyes were on Yan and on the people running out of it as if their lives depended on it – which they did. "It will take them all afternoon to find and question the survivors coming from the city – maybe longer if people choose to hide instead of fleeing the dragon's back."

"They won't," Marielle said. "Not after the past three days."

Etienne had helped them tear down the dam and shoot out of the city. Marielle was a little surprised by that, but Etienne's face had been grim when he met them there.

"We need to be ahead of the news," he'd said without preamble as if he'd thought this whole thing through. "The city leaders will be scared and intimidated by the arrival of a new dragon. They'll send their military forces to take the city and round up the refugees within. The population in the city will be terrified. We need to be out of the city before they arrive if we don't want to be caught up in a sea of interviews and then quietly stashed somewhere."

"I have a letter from the Captain we met in Choan," Marielle said. "It asks them to give us access to the dragon."

"Good," Etienne had said as he covered Tamerlan with a tarp. Tamerlan moaned softly, but his eyes never even opened. "But even with a letter, our captive looks suspicious."

Marielle nodded at that, but as she straightened and forced herself to remain calm, she delivered the news. "The dragon here is already dead. But there is another – somewhere. And I don't know where."

The disappointment in Etienne's eyes matched hers perfectly. He froze for just a moment, inhaled and then nodded.

"Any guesses?"

"My Windrose is hurting again. It's probably leading us to the dragon."

"It led her to the guards gathering in Choan," Jhinn said quietly. "I learned that it's better to listen to it."

Etienne was already nodding. "Tell us if it gets more specific."

He ripped the board out of the dam – the one they'd placed just in that place so you could remove it and it would flood all the canals – and then they were shooting the rapids on the forefront of the flood of water, and racing down the canals and out into the sea.

I'll give you a little time, Yan said in Marielle's mind. *I need the rest, anyway.*

And in less than an hour from when Yan landed, they were off his back, out of the city of Yan and in this strange river, dodging between ships and boats and the terrified looks of strangers as they angled toward the city. Marielle patted her belt pouch and hoped that the officials in the towering city above them would listen to the letter and let them in.

The city called to her, pulling at the windrose on her chest and demanding that she enter it. All she could do was hope that her answers lay within.

"Sit low in the boat," Jhinn suggested. "I look like the people here, but you both look like foreigners."

Around them, people in other boats pointed at them and called out in thickly accented voices. But they spoke the same language despite the accent. Marielle wouldn't have guessed that was true.

Marielle squatted down beside Tamerlan, lifting the edge of the tarp to check on him. He drowsed fitfully, jerking and moaning, his head as hot as a forge. There was nothing that could be done for him. Her only hope was that she could find Ram's avatar in time to kill it and free his mind.

"I think you should take the chains off," she whispered to Etienne. "We aren't going to be able to march him around the city with them on and he isn't even thinking straight – not with this fever. I doubt he could attack us."

Etienne looked skeptical. "I wouldn't underestimate him, if I were you. Even raving mad and almost dead, he can do an enormous amount of damage." He looked around them at the hostile, concerned foreigners and sighed. "I see your point."

He ducked under the tarp and a few moments later she heard the sound of metal sliding against metal as he dragged the chains off Tamerlan. He resurfaced as they were nearing the locks that led up to the city.

"I bound his hands behind his back with rawhide. At least that should hold for long enough to draw a sword if he decides to attack."

Who would have thought a few months ago that the ruler of Jingen would be so nervous around an alchemist's apprentice? And who would have thought she would be in love with one even after he tried to kill her and then snapped her mother's neck?

She swallowed down the horror of those thoughts. That wasn't Tamerlan. That was Ram.

And yet, sometimes it was hard to sort through exactly how complicated all of this was. She shook her head and kept her gaze forward.

Stay focused, Marielle.

She ignored how her breath hitched whenever she thought of Tamerlan. She had to keep hoping. She had to keep trying.

Above them, eggs on the ends of ribbons hung across the entry to the locks. They were laced on the railings of ships, painted so brightly that they hardly looked real.

As they approached the choke of the part of the river that fed into the locks, they joined dozens of other small boats seeking entry and Marielle was relieved to see that the styles of boats and the dress of the people entering the city were varied and strange looking. Good. They would not be the only visitors to the city. Perhaps, they would even slip within the gates.

Unfortunately, she could smell apprehension and anxiety in the air around them as people's gazes kept creeping back to Yan lying near their city. Low murmurs and lined brows were everywhere. Fair enough. Dragons didn't just show up and fall asleep next to your city. These people would be crazy if they *weren't* anxious about it.

Jhinn kept them in the center of the mass of boats, as if he could keep hidden in plain sight.

"All boats will pass through the Offices of Inspections once they enter the city," the operator called from the wheelhouse of the lock operator's shed. He said it in the bored way of someone who did this a thousand times a day. Beside him, the other operator wasn't paying attention at all, his eyes looking past them to the novelty of the dragon and the surging waves of soldiers disembarking around it.

They were waved ahead hurriedly and the small boats jostled for position to move into the lock. Jhinn sped deftly between larger boats, ignoring the curses of other boatmen.

Marielle held her breath as the water filled the lock and lifted them up. So far, so good. They spoke the same language. They used canals, too. She could do this. It was far from home, but not so far that she couldn't find her way.

Breathe, Marielle breathe.

They rose up four levels of locks, one by one, in the middle of the jostling masses of boats. Etienne joined her in the bow, looking up tensely as they rose into the city.

"Strange how similar they are to us, and yet how different, don't you think?" Etienne asked.

"Are they different?" Marielle asked. "It hardly even seems so."

Etienne looked at her blandly. "I suppose you are distracted."

The burning in her chest was intensifying. But he was right. The fashions around them, the patterns of speech – too quick in parts and drawling in others – the formal way that the lock operators spoke and moved, the lack of family boats but increase in trade vessels that were clearly foreign – it was all different. But they were still just people living in a city, with the threat of Legends and dragons hanging over their heads. And that was something she could relate to.

"I suppose you are right," Marielle conceded as they reached the final lock, and were disgorged on the other side.

The boats around them spread out, and before them rose the solidified, dead dragon with the city built on top of it. On its back, the city rose up glorious and powerful, molding itself to scales and wings and tail, bright and bustling, straining with activity and music and bright decoration. The architecture foreign in its curves, planes, and open-topped buildings, but breathtakingly beautiful.

And at its very center, as if in celebration of the holiday, a golden egg as large as a castle was nestled, the city wrapped around it protectively.

The windrose in Marielle's chest flared with so much heat that she stumbled.

"That's it," she gasped, pointing at the egg. "That's what we're looking for."

31: WHISPER

He was clinging to consciousness.

Give in, Ram urged. But he'd bested the Legend again and his mind was his own for now – what was left of it. His thoughts felt as slippery as the fish Jhinn would throw into the gondola as he reset his lines. They leapt and jumped and when he tried to catch them, they slipped away.

He would not give in.

Give in to what?

Marielle's face swam into view. He tried to reach up and touch her, but his hands wouldn't move. Something bit painfully into his wrist.

"Marielle?" he croaked. His throat was dry. He saw the look of concern in her eyes and a moment later, she was pouring cold water over his lips. Just a trickle, and he could barely keep up to choke it down.

He coughed and sputtered. Gasping for air. It felt like his lungs couldn't suck it in.

You are dying. As soon as you slip, I will have you. I can live long past the time you would die. The moment you give in, this body will be mine.

He had to warn her.

"Marielle." It came out as a whisper, but she heard him. Her purple eyes were close to his. One of them was slowly turning a milky white.

"It's okay," she whispered. "Lie still. Etienne is talking to the guards. He has the letter."

"You have to hurry," Tamerlan whispered.

"We will. We'll get you somewhere safe."

"No!" it was barely loud enough to hear. "Ram almost has me. I can't hold on much longer. If he takes me over, then he will take this body forever."

Her forehead wrinkled.

"Kill me now," he gasped.

"I can't," she whispered back, looking up and around her frantically before looking down on him with tear-filled eyes. "Don't ask me to do what I can't."

Maybe there were guards around. She'd mentioned guards, hadn't she?

"Please hang on," she whispered.

"Sunset," he gasped, his mangled chest an aching mass of pain. "I'll try to stay alive until sunset."

The sun was hanging low in the late afternoon sky. He could give her that long at least – couldn't he? He'd read stories about people surviving on will alone. He would have to do the same. At least until sunset.

"You have to know," he whispered.

"Know what?" She put her ear to his mouth as if she could barely hear it. The touch of her skin against his lips sent shudders of happiness through him. One last kiss. One last moment of tenderness. He wanted to savor it forever, but he had to tell her.

"If I die, he'll take my body. Ram. He won't die, too. And then you'll have to kill him quickly. I'm keeping him weak by being here. With me gone, he'll be powerful again."

She started to pull away. His strength was fading.

"Wait!" he begged and she paused. He kissed her ear and whispered. "I love you forever. Don't be afraid to do what you must."

Blackness took him again.

32: EGG OF DRAGONS

MARIELLE

Marielle felt cold all over as Jhinn pulled away from the guard station.

"Etienne says they're letting us into the city but they're asking him to report to the Nine Seas Palace on our behalf. We need to report back to this guard station in one day to retrieve him or be taken into custody if they don't like what he says on our behalf," Marielle told Jhinn.

"And if we don't," Jhinn asked, and she shot him a worried look. He was going to get them taken in right now, and she couldn't afford that!

"If we don't, then we'll be wanted by the City Watch, the Palace Guard and all the Gate Guards, which will make life here exceptionally difficult," she said, trying not to snap. "Can you angle us toward that huge egg in the middle of the city?"

She was watching the sun as it sank in the sky. It was so close to the horizon. They might not even have an hour before it dipped below the horizon of the sea in the west. She licked her lips nervously. Tamerlan had sunk into oblivion after giving her his dire warning. And that had been an hour ago. They'd lost a lot of time talking to the authorities. Would they have enough time?

"If I can't get to that egg, then I'm not much of a boatman," Jhinn said. "The canal leads straight toward it."

"Good," Marielle said. "I have until sunset to get there and find Ram's avatar."

"What do you think his avatar is?" Jhinn asked.

"I have no idea."

"And you think you only have until sunset to find it?" he sounded like she was mad.

Maybe she was. Wasn't this whole thing an insane endeavor? Wasn't she crazy to try to do it at all?

"Just get me there, and we'll worry about that later," she said, reaching down to smooth Tamerlan's sweaty hair from his brow. "Hold on, Tamerlan. Fight for a little longer."

They slid through the crowd of boats, Jhinn's pedals whirring as he carried them to the heart of the city. If Marielle hadn't been frantic, she would have been in awe. Massive columns soared into the sky, topped with sculptures of ships on the high seas and people stepping out of the waves. Wide terraces close to the canals were filled with people dressed in the corals, pinks, and oranges of Springhatch and carrying heaping trays of delectable foods shaped to look like eggs. Was it Springhatch already?

The sounds of the city were nervous, matching the edgy, wary scent of the people as they gazed into the distance at the dragon that had landed on their shores. But despite that, they eventually settled into the coming evening, even slipping occasionally into laughter.

By their clothing and the nervous parties starting all around them, it was definitely Springhatch. And it was unlucky not to celebrate it.

Perhaps her own future was going to end on the day when the world celebrated fertility and life.

She tried not to think of that as the sun slowly sunk lower and lower and they pushed their way between crowded boats.

"Did you see that dragon descend?" someone laughed in a boat nearby, and her ears pricked up as she listened for an answer.

"I was so shocked! I could barely go to the docks for the fish. We all wanted to go and see the dragon, but you know what the Qui'Reign said."

There was a murmur of agreement from around that voice. What was a Qui'Reign?

And then someone else spoke. "If our great leader can bring a dragon down from the sky and pin it there while our soldiers go to bind it, then imagine what else she can do? We'll have to stop complaining about taxation!"

"Shhh! Be silent, Ta'vor. You're drunk!"

The speakers looked around them warily and Marielle kept her eyes on the egg, pretending not to hear or understand.

If these common people were right and the soldiers were trying to bind Yan, then she needed to hurry even more.

Bind me? Never!

She heard a distant roar and flinched. Hopefully, the refugees had all fled the city. If they hadn't, it was too late, now!

"Almost there," Jhinn murmured.

The Egg was so large that they could only see the underside of it now except for where it rested in a carefully woven metal net. It was as if someone had made a net of wrist-thick black metal strands and rested the egg inside. The strands ended in bold claws that gripped the egg. The structure rose up out of the water, black and tangled around the perfect, golden egg. The water reflected the gold beautifully, one shining surface identical to the other. It was breathtaking.

The surface of the egg was a light gold color, speckled with darker gold spots, irregular and of every size, almost like a speckled chicken's egg.

It couldn't be a real dragon's egg – could it?

It feels wrong. Not just like an egg, but as if someone sealed an egg in stasis, Yan said. But who would do that?

Ram the Hunter. He would do that.

There was a moan in the distance, barely audible, and yet it made the ground tremble as if a great creature had made the sound.

Marielle felt a chill of dread creeping up through her throat, leaving her sick and nauseated. And if he'd frozen the egg, somehow, then maybe it was tied to his avatar. But how – where – would she find that avatar?

"Pull up to the egg," she said to Jhinn.

She thought she might be able to climb up the woven metal and stand with the egg in the basket above the water, but as she watched it, considering what to do, she was almost knocked over as Tamerlan stood up, snapped his bonds, and leapt to the egg.

33: Breaking of an Avatar

He was barely holding on. Pain leaked from him in every direction. He gasped in and out of his hold on himself, Ram shaking it from him by fits and turns, but he wasn't going to die in the grips of the Legend. Not if he could help it.

Back when the recipe had slipped from the pages of that old book on Summernight, he never imagined that this would be the result.

"For dire situations," it had said. "for the summoning of the ancient powers."

He'd been such a fool to think that an alchemist's apprentice could delve into all of that. It hadn't even been a year, and those same powers had ruined him, crumbling him bit by bit until all that was left of him was this blood-stained scrap of a human, still craving the very spices that had driven him to this moment.

Ram ripped through his strength and stole his body, leaping up despite pain that would have crippled Tamerlan and leaping past Marielle to climb up a ladder-like basket of woven metal. It looked like an art piece – if you wove art out of the metal rib cages of giants.

Pain seared through him as Ram found what he was looking for – a single dull red mark on the surface of the bright golden egg. He couldn't hide from Tamerlan what he was looking at.

I don't need to hide anything. This is the end. We end this here.

He spun, crouched in front of the egg as Marielle scaled the nest after him, slanting her climb so that she could mount the platform out of his reach. Wise. She'd grown so wise since he first met her.

Still his perfect nemesis. Still the one person who could end all of this. He could remember when he first met her in his dark room. She'd been so vulnerable and yet so in charge – hunting him, looking for him, ready to capture this threat to her world. If only she had.

Focus. Your wandering mind distracts from what we do here.

He wasn't going to kill Marielle. Never.

It was a relief that he didn't have a weapon.

Beyond them, this foreign city celebrated, sleepy and safe in the sure knowledge that nothing could hurt them while here – at the heart of it –that which had started months ago finally came to a head.

Focus.

Ram reached out and up and grabbed one of the steel claws holding the egg, snapping the tip off and brandishing it in his hand as he crouched once more before the egg.

How did he do those things? How did he use Tamerlan's body to accomplish things he'd never be able to do on his own?

Magic. It's all been magic. The ancient blood magic of our people before we brought the dragons.

There was no blood here.

Ram reached down and touched Tamerlan's side and then held up his hand, slick with the blood leaking out of him.

It's always been your blood, Tamerlan. We've been feeding off your life since the first time you called us, and Lila took you as her plaything. I'll draw off of it until you collapse. But before you do, we will conquer.

"Tamerlan?" Marielle called.

Yes. She will be the avatar.

Tamerlan pushed back against him, but Ram held him at bay, holding out the claw.

"You'll have to come for me, little woman. And with my hands unbound and a weapon in them, you can't win. I can overpower you. I can fight through pain you can't survive. You can carve this body limb from limb and you won't beat me — can't beat me. I will win this."

Despair washed over Tamerlan at the truth echoing in the Legend's words. He didn't have the power to stop him.

But he had to try.

With the last of his strength, he battered at the wall.

"You're protecting your avatar, Ram," Marielle said with a glint in her eye. "It's the shell, isn't it? You had to seal that baby dragon in the egg somehow – after you'd bound all the rest."

"Do you know how hard it is to bind a dragon? To find a person willing to give their life to be what binds them?" Ram asked her. "I thought I'd won, and then I found this. The things they had to do to me to make this golden shell … they'd haunt your nightmares for centuries if you knew. I know they haunted mine. They don't consider me unspeakable for no reason."

Her eyes were scanning his every twitch, looking for a weakness, looking to throw him off.

Tamerlan wanted to plead with her to leave, to run, to never return. He could feel Ram tensing, ready to destroy her and there was no way to stop him.

A spark flashed in her eye. Understanding and … scheming?

"That red spot is the vulnerability in the shell, isn't it?" she said, so loudly that Tamerlan was surprised that the city didn't freeze at her words. She took a step back as if reconsidering.

"It doesn't matter if you know," Ram said. "You won't survive this fight. And there is no one else here. You should have waited for your pretty friend in black. Maybe he would have backed you up."

She took another step back, fear in her eyes now, and Ram took a step forward, following her.

"You can't escape me now," he said.

Her sword was up, and she stabbed it toward him, fast as a viper.

Yes! Fight, Marielle! Fight to kill!

Fool! Always, you try to sabotage the inevitable.

He deflected her thrust easily and lunged toward her with the metal claw, slashing but missing as she leapt backward. She'd duped him, not fully committed to the thrust but ready the whole time to dart backward.

She knows she is weaker. She should not have come to this place. I can access more magic here. I will make her an avatar and trap that dragon Yan on this very platform. See how she already weakens?

She was moving slower as she parried his next slash, backing up, but not as quickly as before as if she were tiring.

Please, Marielle! Please hold on or flee. This enemy is too great for you!

Even as he battled, he could feel his strength slipping away. They were on the other side of the egg from the red spot now. Marielle stumbled and Ram lunged at her.

Tamerlan wanted to shut his eyes. He didn't want to watch her eyes widening as the metal claw arced through the air toward her, didn't want to feel his own muscles betraying him as they threw all their force behind the blow, didn't want to hear her moan of pain as the claw slid across her ribs or feel Ram raising the claw again for another blow.

He didn't want to watch her die.

And he didn't have to – yet.

Ram fell to his knees with a cry of agony.

Why? They hadn't been hit.

Tamerlan shoved hard with every ounce of remaining strength. It shouldn't have been enough, but it was enough. He had his body back!

He threw the claw into the water. His jaw slackening in surprise at the look of triumph in Marielle's eyes.

What – ?

"It didn't work, Marielle!" Jhinn's voice called. He was on the platform! On the other side.

Tamerlan gasped. No wonder Marielle looked triumphant. She'd led Ram away from that spot on purpose!

"Jhinn," he gasped.

Marielle nodded grimly. "He's willing to make the sacrifice – for his people. For all the people."

"Please, Marielle. You need to kill me this time," it came out in a rush. "You don't need to feel guilty and you don't need to keep fighting it."

He stepped forward, kissed her tenderly, a hot searing kiss filled with all the promises he'd never be able to make, all the hurts he'd never be able to take away and all the love he had left in his breaking heart. He reached down with his wounded hand and pulled her sword blade to his chest. Tears traced down her cheeks and her lower lip trembled.

"I can't, Tamerlan."

"It's okay, Marielle. It's okay," he put all his confidence into his smile, all his love. "It's for the best. You're doing the right thing. I – "

Tamerlan fell backward, slamming onto the metal of the basket and sliding to his knees. Something was hammering at the metal of the egg, reverberating through the whole thing. He heard something smash.

"It's working!" Jhinn called.

Ram overwhelmed him, taking his body. He tried to scream as his control was taken, but it came out as a grunt.

"Wait. It stopped," Jhinn said, anxiety in his voice. "I thought we had it, but it's like the avatar broke and then resurfaced."

"It has a new vessel," Marielle said grimly, and Tamerlan felt the tip of her sword pressing against his chest.

Yes!

Do, it, Marielle! Do it!

32: Deliverer of Death

"Just like Anglarok and Liandari," Jhinn sighed.

Marielle didn't feel like sighing. She felt like wailing.

She'd come so far. She'd been so close. She'd tricked Ram. They'd killed his avatar.

And none of it had been enough.

Her vision blurred as hot tears welled up and spilled down her cheeks. The point of her sword pressed against Tamerlan's chest, digging into his clothing deep enough that red blood was welling up and staining the cloth. Ram's eyes were locked on hers, defying her to push the blade through his chest.

"Tamerlan knew this was coming," Jhinn said gently. He'd circled the egg to be close to her. "He told us what to do."

But it wasn't supposed to end like this. It was supposed to end with her finding a way to *save* him. It was supposed to end with the sweet Tamerlan back – the one who loved her and who cared about orphans on the streets. The one who was willing to risk everything to save the life of someone he didn't know.

But happy endings weren't the only endings.

And this one wasn't going to be happy.

She clenched her jaw, steeled her nerve and drew the blade back to get enough force to strike.

Ram moved like a serpent, sliding away from her strike, his back to the egg still as he reached up to grab another claw-like point of the nest.

Jhinn charged with the hammer, trying to hit him but Ram was too strong even now. He let go of the claw he was trying to rend apart, grabbed Jhinn by the arm with one hand and tossed him aside like a rag doll. He flew through the air, past the nest to the canal beyond.

But Jhinn had given her just enough time.

As Ram was still tossing him, she charged.

Her blade slid between his ribs and through his heart. She grabbed the pommel of the sword with both hands, sobbing as she threw all her weight behind it and shoved with all her upper body strength, pushing through her hips until every ounce of weight was in her blow.

The blade met resistance, but she felt it slicing flesh, cleaving bone, and then on the other side, spearing through the eggshell behind him.

She gasped, staggering backward and leaving the sword in his chest. She was watching the eyes. She saw the moment that Ram left and only Tamerlan remained, coughing blood and gasping, pinned to the egg.

"Good," he gasped. "Good work."

He tried to reach to her, but all that moved was a single finger.

She rushed to him, reaching out to hold him around the sword. She was choking, too. She was choking on tears and agonizing grief. She'd killed him in the end. Just like she'd feared. Just like he knew she would.

"Tam," she managed between sobs. "I'm so sorry."

He coughed blood. His words were wet and thick. "Love you alw —"

"No, no, no," she said, shaking, breaking apart. Her chest heaved as the sobs wracked her and she fell against his chest, not bothering to disguise her grief as it tore through her.

Above her, she heard a crack.

The egg was hatching.

All of this for dragons she'd never meet. For people she didn't know.

Tamerlan slumped forward as the sword fell from the egg. Marielle caught him, stumbling back and to the ground. She wrenched the sword from his chest and threw it away. She didn't want to see another sword as long as she lived. She didn't want to live.

She lifted him from the neat and cradled him in her arms as the cracks continued, staring at his open, glassy eye, caressing his hair and face as gently as a mother with a baby.

There were shouts on the shore and even screams and Jhinn was calling something up to her, but her eyes were thick with tears and all she could see was Tamerlan's golden scent drifting away in the breeze.

With every breath, there was less of him in the air. As if he'd never existed at all.

And she couldn't help herself. She couldn't be strong anymore. She couldn't care about what was happening to the city or to Yan, to Jhinn or to Etienne. All she could do was sob and sob over her dead, wishing it had been different. Wishing she could go back to when she'd talked to him in his room at the Alchemist's Guild all those months ago and wishing she could haul him off to the guardhouse and lock him up and get her throat cut over the dragon like Etienne had planned, because then he'd be alive. Wishing she could do it all over again and do it differently. Wishing she'd been able to save him.

A crack sounded this time that was so loud, that she finally looked up, blinking tears back just enough to see.

The top of the egg shoved up, a chunk of it sliding to the side and falling to smash on the metal basket on the other side of the egg. The nest rocked wildly.

A split ran down the side of the egg, directly where she was, thick silver fluid leaking out of it. A head about the size of her body popped up through the missing piece of the egg, wet and gleaming, its golden eye glittering in the last shreds of sunset light.

Something had hatched on Springhatch.

The hatchling let out a long keening sound, and then the top half of the egg shattered, pieces flying in every direction. It was like a dam burst. Silver fluid poured out of the top half of the egg, thick and viscous. It washed over her and Tamerlan like someone had thrown a bucket of it over them, drenching them completely.

The water of Life. Jhinn talked about it all the time, and she was seeing it, wasn't she? Just like the waters between worlds, this water in the egg had sustained that baby dragon all this time.

As the young dragon rose into the air, flapping sopping wet wings in the dusky night, and sending a rain of life water over the streets around them, a silver beam shot up from the egg and expanded until it dwarfed the city, shining more brightly than the sun.

A portal – identical to the one they'd seen in the mountains – opened where the egg had been. Water that was not water poured out of it in a flood, washing over her and her dead. The flow was so powerful that she scrambled to get out of the flow and to the space of air under it, as under a waterfall, pulling Tamerlan with her. She couldn't give him up. She wouldn't. She wrapped her arms around his remains, clasping his face to her chest under the waterfall. She let the water wash all around her as she shivered under it. She should get out. She should go find Jhinn. She should do something.

But all she could do was shiver under the waterfall and stare at all this supposed life with her one good eye while the one person whose life was precious to her lay lifeless in her arms.

Water washed over and over and over them until they were soaked with it. The scent of it so overpowering that it was all she could smell now. It smelled of spring rains and turned earth, of growing grass and spring breezes. It smelled of new life.

She gasped in a breath of it.

Tamerlan moaned.

Marielle almost dropped him as a gasp caught in her throat. She began to shake, her teeth chattering together. She didn't dare look at his face. Hope was too much for the despairing. It broke you and broke you until you heard what you wanted to hear.

She risked a glance at his face, afraid to look and feel disappointment stab through her again.

His eye fluttered open.

Oh.

Oh, sweet dragons.

Her breathing was so fast she couldn't catch a breath. Her heart thudding in her chest like a dozen horses racing.

She clung to him, gasping until she could speak.

"Tamerlan? Is that … you?"

His smile as he looked up at her was radiant.

She choked back a sob, and now she was really crying, her hands caressing his face and her breathing ragged as she her words tumbled out.

"You're alive, you're alive!"

"Marielle," he said, but whatever else he might have said, she didn't know, because her lips sought his and she kissed him, channeling all her fears and hopes, all the desperate longings she had that this was really true into that one kiss. She clung to him, her hand that had been holding them in place snaked around to hold his waist instead, drawing him closer as she frantically kissed him.

Maybe she had gone mad, too. Maybe none of this was real. But if it was a dream, she never wanted to wake up. If it was madness, she didn't want a cure.

They washed out from under the falls, sweeping through the rushing portal water, tangled in each other's embrace and then flying through the air.

She fell on something hard but padded, and Jhinn's frustrated curse finally brought her head up.

"Still not dead, boy?" he said roughly as she drew back from Tamerlan just enough to look at him again.

She didn't care what Jhinn thought. She didn't care about anything beyond this moment.

She let her eyes run all over Tamerlan. The bloody wound at his side – and the other one through his ribs – were gone. The fabric of his clothing was still torn and stained there, but the flesh was whole. She touched her hand to it in wonder, words spilling from her lips.

"I'm so sorry, Tamerlan. I'm so sorry. I had to do it. I – "

He kissed her again and cut off her words, laughing when he pulled back, his face filled with assurance and love.

"You saved me, Marielle. You saved us all."

"But I put a sword through your chest!" she protested. "How are you still alive?"

"I told you," Jhinn said reverently. "Water is life. And the water flowing from that portal brought him back to life. And now look. Stop kissing and thinking you're both so amazing and *look*."

Yan was circling above Xytexyx, the new hatchling at his side. They looped tight circles around the city four times while the people gasped in amazement. Marielle gasped right with them, but her hands found Tamerlan's and her fingers threaded through his. She wasn't willing to let go of him. Not now, not ever, not even for the sight of a lifetime.

She stole little glances at his face to watch his reaction and felt heat creep over her whenever her gaze brushed over his doing the same.

Yan and the hatchling took a final loop and then dove through the moon-like portal and were lost in the bright light. Around them, the city roared, a great cheer rising up from thousands of throats.

Marielle held her breath and then the portal began to close and the water started to flow into it instead of out of it. Jhinn pedaled frantically to the nearest canal lip. And pointed to it as the gondola crashed against the stone.

"This is where you get out," he said, tension in every word. "I need to go through before it closes."

Marielle gaped at him, but Tamerlan was quick to nod, dragging Marielle out of the gondola to the shore.

"Thank you, my friend," he said sincerely to Jhinn, catching him in a quick embrace. "For everything."

Jhinn caught Marielle's eye with a smile on his lips.

"Redemption," he said, simply. "All is forgiven, I think. For both of us."

And then he was angling the gondola to the sucking water being pulled back into the portal. He leaned forward, pedaling hard, his eyes fixed on the gap ahead. The little craft sped upward into the falls while the people around them gasped. Jhinn had to duck low as the portal nearly closed on him, but he made it. He turned, finally, and she could just see him wave to them, winking as the portal shut, the light extinguished and darkness descended in the city of Xytexyx.

It was done.

No more Legends.

No more Dragons.

EPILOGUE: GIFTS MAKE A GIVER

TAMERLAN

Sometimes, on days like this, when everything was happy, he wondered if he'd really been raised from the dead or if this was the life after. Because if this turned out to be what came after, then he wouldn't be surprised. Because it was perfect.

His mind was gloriously free. So free, and so quiet, that sometimes when no one else was around, he wept with the sheer relief of it. His body was his own. His mind was his own. If he did something wrong, it was only his own choices to blame. If he did something right … well, he'd done a lot right. And he'd do a lot more right yet.

Because that was the beauty of life. As long as you were breathing, every minute you had left, was a minute to make the right choice. A minute to save someone else. A minute to treasure what you had.

"Tam!" a little voice called, and he looked down to see Sabrin holding up one of his brown rabbits in his little hands, his eyes very grave. "Can you hold Mr. Acorn while I go and play."

"Of course I can," Tamerlan said, gathering the fluffy rabbit into his arms and tussling Sabrin's hair as the child ran to join his friends kicking a whicker around in the long dirt street.

Their streets didn't have gondolas and canals anymore. And every time that Tamerlan walked up and down the peculiarly straight, dusty streets, his heart would feel a little pang at the reminder that they were the poorer for the lack of them. He'd never see Jhinn again, never sleep in the bottom of a boat or brew tea over a swinging brazier in a boat. The lack of canals reminded him of that every day.

Whenever the moon was full in the sky, Tamerlan always found himself pausing and staring at it and remembering when the boy from the water had gone up to live forever in the space between the stars, through a portal that looked like the moon.

But Etienne had been right to order the streets be made broad and straight. With all the traffic coming into the City of Velendark from the mountains and the sea, and the landholds around the city, even these wide streets were hardly wide enough.

The former Lord Mythos had named the city after himself – of course. Just like Allegra had named her city Spellspinner. And though the cities were friendly, they disputed the details of how to split the Dragonblood Plains almost as often as their founders disputed things. And they made up again just as quickly. Tamerlan was fairly sure that Etienne was in Spellspinner as often as he was in Velendark, though he only saw the ruler occasionally when Marielle convinced him to join her for a party in the brand new palace, or when he had to go and ask Etienne for funding for the orphanage. The Lord Mhythos always gave Tamerlan what he asked for with a look in his eye that made Tamerlan's heart freeze. No one else on the Dragonblood Plains knew who he was. And Marielle didn't care. But Etienne knew and he would never forget. He watched Tamerlan like you might watch a dragon sleeping beneath your city who could rise at any time. And he always said yes, as if he were wary about saying no.

He shivered. His hands still twitched sometimes, thinking of power and his lungs longed for the smoke of the spice. Because although they'd slain the Legends they knew about, Tamerlan wasn't entirely convinced that there weren't more across the Bridge. And if he ever slipped – if he ever ground up that recipe of spices again – he might call new Legends and ruin everything. Marielle had tried to give him a mortar and pestle for Summernight – not the same Summernight as they used to have. They gave gifts on this Summernight and Etienne gave a speech about wrong assumptions and heroism in honor of Marielle. And most importantly no one was slaughtered. Tamerlan had hidden the pestle and mortar in the cellar, but a few nights later he'd gone down there, hands twitching and mind racing, wanting him to blend the spice and call the Legends. Instead, he'd taken the fine items, shoved them in a sack and tossed them in the river. Never again.

He stood and stared so often at the moon or at the river that the children of Waters of Life Orphange sometimes called Tamerlan 'Moonman.' And he didn't mind that at all.

There were forty-two children in the big house. He'd gathered them one by one from the ruins of the old cities and the gutters of the refugee camps. Children with no homes or families left. Children who'd had no hope – until now. They'd been reborn into a new hope, just like him. And he loved every one of them for it.

And most days, when Marielle came home from her day as Captain of the Velendark City Scenters, she brought another child with her. Even after a year, there were still refugees and orphans trickling into the new cities. All of them looking for a place to call home again. All of them needing someone to care about them. And for once in his life, Tamerlan's big heart wasn't a hinderance.

He turned at the sound of a low laugh and saw Marielle lowering her face-veil to smile at him, the patch over her eye matched her smart leather uniform.

"How is Mr. Acorn today?" she asked with a look at the rabbit and a smirk that made her face alive and vibrant.

"He seems fine, Captain Zi'fen," Tamerlan said, meeting her smirk with a soft look of affection. "How is our fine city?"

"Getting finer," Marielle said. "If we can sort out this dispute between he Alchemists and the Librarians over who gets the haul of books we found in a library that fell from H'yi's back into a swamp to the west of here."

Tamerlan laughed. "Any good books left over?"

Marielle pulled a hand from behind her back. She was holding a small leather tome entitled, *Birds of the Dragonblood Plains*.

"This particular book went missing from the stash," she said with a grin. "I thought maybe you could take care of it for a while. It would be a shame if the Librarians or the Alchemists tore it in their fight to keep all the books for themselves."

And after that poor Mr. Acorn had to fend for himself in the grass around their feet as Tamerlan pulled his wife into his arms and very thoroughly kissed her, wondering again at how everyone could say that magic had left the world when every day seemed so richly magical to him.

BEHIND THE SCENES:

USA Today bestselling author, Sarah K. L. Wilson loves spinning a yarn and if it paints a magical new world, twists something old into something reborn, or makes your heart pound with excitement ... all the better! Sarah hails from the rocky Canadian Shield in Northern Ontario - learning patience and tenacity from the long months of icy cold - where she lives with her husband and two small boys. You might find her building fires in her woodstove and wishing she had a dragon handy to light them for her

Sarah would like to thank **Eugenia Kollia** for her incredible work in proofreading this book. Without her big heart and passion for stories, this book would not be the same.

Sarah has the deepest regard for the talent of her phenomenal artists – **Francesca Baerald** who designed the gorgeous map for this series and Lius Lasahido and his team at **Polar Engine** who created the gorgeous cover art that accompanies this book. Without their work, it would be so much harder to show off this story the way it deserves!

www.sarahklwilson.com